I0579837

This is a work of fiction. Names, characters, places, and incidents either are the product of the author's imagination or are used fictitiously. Any resemblance to actual events, locales, organizations, or persons, living or dead, is entirely coincidental and beyond the intent of either the author or the publisher.

Wishing Thinking: a Club Raven novel
By Kiernan Kelly
Copyright © 2017

Evil Plot Bunny LLC
PO Box 722
Loughman, FL 33858

Cover illustration by Erin Dameron-Hill
Published with permission

ISBN: 978-1-942831-40-2

Wishing Thinking
A Club Raven Novel
by Kiernan Kelly

Wishing Thinking: A Club Raven Novel

Wishing Thinking

Wishful Thinking: a Club Raven Novel
By Kiernan Kelly

Prologue

A gust of wind whistled in from the bayacross the muddy road, fragrant from the sea but frightfully sharp. It bit Tony's face, and he shivered despite his double-breasted frock coat, gloves, and beaver fur-felt top hat. For a moment, he urgently wished for a closed buggy ride back to Club Raven, where a cheerfully blazing fire was no doubt warming the great room, and a snifter of brandy in a fine crystal glass awaited him. He pushed the thought away with an effort; not even the wet chill of an October night at the Baltimore wharfs could chase him away from his post. He'd spent too much time and effort arranging for his quarry to be here in this place, at this hour, to give up on his plans now.

A small, sad sigh escaped his lips as his longing for a brandy and a fire faded but refused to completely die. To distract himself, he focused for a moment on the head of his walking stick, a solid gold tiger, and how it glinted in the moonlight. It was the fanciest walking stick he could find, and cost more money than he'd seen at one time. Well, before he was chosen as one of three heirs to Club Raven, that is. Now, he was richer than anyone he'd ever known, with the exception of the other two owners. The stick was a symbol of his new station in life, and how he saw himself—a sturdy, solid shaft that otherwise might've ended its life as no more than kindling, now given a new incarnation by the glittering, golden idol attached to it. He shifted the walking stick to his other hand and returned his attention to the wharf. He whistled a jaunty little tune to keep his mind off the chill as he waited.

He stilled when he spotted two figures silhouetted against the darker shapes of ships moored at the dock, and his mouth quirked in a predatory smile. This was them, the two men he'd met in New York just six weeks ago—although "met" wasn't precisely how most people would describe their first encounter. The memory washed over him, and he could practically smell the odor of the congested street in Five Points.

Mulberry Bend is exactly as he remembers it. The street is spotted with horse dung and refuse, clogged with buggies, carts, horses and people, the noise they make a constant rumble. Buildings squashed together side-by-side, their stoops claimed by ragged children holding equally ragged dolls, orplaying at hoops on the sidewalk,or by men loitering in rough, homespun shirts and patched trousers. Women lean out of windows, hanging graying laundry on lines strung from one building to the next. A deep breath brings a lungful of onion, garlic, fish, body odor, and sewage, the reek so thick he can practically taste it. One whiff reignites Tony's gratitude to his benefactor for giving him a way out of Five Points that didn't end with him in a casket.

His cab, an open-air buggy pulled by a slat-sided horse, is stalled by the traffic. Tony leans forward and taps his driver's shoulder. "I'll walk from here."

The cabbie twists around to look at him, eyes wide. "But sir, this is Five Points. Ain't no place for a gentleman. It's dangerous."

He passes a coin to the driver. "Ha! Not for me. I grew up here. Wait for me at the far end of Baxter. I'll be along directly." The driver tips his cap, albeit reluctantly, as Tony exits the buggy to the street.

The first storefront he comes to is the cobbler's shop belonging to Abram Weiss. Tony smiles. He remembers his mama taking him to see Mr. Weiss, a gruff old man with a long white beard, to have new soles put on Tony's shoes. He peers through the dusty window. A man his own age sits amid a clutter of shoes, tapping at a boot's sole with a tiny hammer. Weiss's son, perhaps. The old man is probably long gone on to his reward by now.

His walking stick clicks on the pavement as he walks away, the golden tiger serving as its handle glinting in the bright sunlight. He can see it draw the attention of passersby; gold is as rare as fairy farts in Five Points, and as tempting to a man with a talent for theft as a banquet to a beggar. No one in his right mind would flash such wealth out in the open on the street— it's an open invitation to thievery.

No one, that is, except Tony. In fact, he is counting on it. He needs to present himself as a victim in order for his plan to succeed.

The other members at Club Raven areall rich. They've had money, lots of it, and either came from fine, upstanding families or earned their reputations through their own accomplishments. Although nothing had ever been directly said, he felt less than the others, as if he were constantly being judged because of his past.

He didn't come from family money, and had few accomplishments to claim except one for pickpocketing. He was born the youngest son of poor, Italian immigrants. His father died when he was an infant, leaving Tony to grow up fatherless in one of the roughest neighborhoods in Manhattan. His entire life seemed one long fight for scraps. Although his talent, his gift, made it a bit easier for him than others, he remembered plenty of nights when he'd gone to bed hungry. The worst memory he had was when his older brother, Salvatore, took sick with consumption. They couldn't afford a doctor or medicine. Watching Salvatore die left him with nightmares that still haunted him.

And that is what brings him back to Five Points today. He is on a mission to find a young man he can aid the same way he'd been helped. In a single act of kindness, he will set in motion a plan to bring the young man he chooses down to Baltimore, and eventually, to Club Raven. Tonyintends to prove he isn't a fluke; that good men aren't necessarily the product of wealth and breeding.

Tony focuses his attention on his surroundings. It won't do to be distracted by memories right now, not unless he wants to actually lose his walking stick to some quick-handed thief.

A man wearing dark spectaclesstands on the corner, holding a small basket full of stubby pencils. Tony realizesthe man is blind and, fishing out his billfold, sticks a dollar in the man's basket before moving on. It never hurts to pass on good fortune when the opportunity arises.

In the middle of the next blockis a grocery. A series of wooden crates brimming with apples, pears, and oranges are neatly lined outside the shop. He stops and lifts a fragrant apple to his nose. As he digs into his pocket for a coin to give the shopkeeper, he notices a redheaded young man dressed in coarse knickers and shirt, wearing a wool ivy cap pulled low over his eyes, hovering just behind him, pretending to examine the fruit.

His hand comes up empty. His pocket ispicked clean; not a single coin remains. A quick search finds his billfold gone as well. Turning, he spots the redhead moving away, pushing quickly through the crowd.

Tony is intrigued. He doesn't doubt the redhead is the thief, but how had he been robbed so effortlessly?The redhead hadn't been close enough to Tony to nick his billfold, had he? Tony drops the apple back into the crate and takes off after the young man.

If it had been another well-to-do man who'd been the redhead's victim, the thief would surely have gotten clean away, but Tony has an advantage most rich men don't—he knows the area as well as he knows his own name. No matter how many alleys the thief turnsinto, or how many fences scaled, or twists and turns taken, Tony doggedly remains on the trail.

In the end, it is Tony's stamina that finally gives out. He is a long time from his days as a boy scrambling to stay alive in Five Points. When the redhead turns into a particularly dark alley—it is called "Bandit's Roost" he remembers, and most appropriately—Tony stops, breathing hard. He curses himself for getting soft, then yells at the thief, allowing his gift to flow through him.

"Stop!"

The redhead in front of him skids to a stop as if yanked by invisible reins. Tony can see the thief's bewilderment as he approaches, breathing heavily. He sticks his hand into the redhead's front pocket and pulls out his billfold. A quick check reveals all his money is still in it. "You're quick, I'll give you that, but how did you manage to pick my pocket from so far away? You were never less than three feet from me." Tony smiles. "Quite an impressive feat, young man."

Panic is etched in the redhead's expression. "What did you do to me? Why can't I move?"

"First things first. My name is Anthony Brazzio, but you can call me Tony. Tell me your name."

"Seamus O'Brian. They call me Bull."

Tony chuckles. Seamus has a sweet Irish lilt, and a fine, sturdy body. His gaze traces the lines of Seamus's stocky physique. "Well, you do look like a burly little redheaded bull. Tell me how you picked my pocket."

He can see Bull fighting the urge to do as Tony demands, and gives him credit for resisting nearly a full half a minute. That is more than most people can do, given the strength of Tony's talent for the power of suggestion. "I have this thing I can do, see? I can move things from one place to another by thinking about it, so long as I know where the thing is. I seen your gold walking stick, and your fancy clothes, and when I saw you take out your billfold from your right breast pocket to give Blind Eddie a dollar, I knew you was rich and probably had lots more where that came from. So, when I got close to you at the grocers, I just pictured your billfold popping out of your pocket and into mine, and...well..."

"And it happened."

"Yeah. Now let me go! You got your money back."

"Can you can move anything, or does it have to be something light, like a billfold?"

"Naw, it only works with small things, like wallets and jewelry and such."

"Handy when you're a pickpocket, hmm?"

Seamus twists, fighting against Tony's invisible bonds again. "Let me go!"

Just then a new voice sounds, and Tony feels a hard push that nearly knocks him to his knees. "This cockchafer causing you problems, Bull?"

Tony spins around and finds himself facing a good-looking young man. The newcomer is dark-haired and dark-eyed, taller and more slender but dressed similarly to Bull, and shares the same charming Irish accent. "Tell me your name."

"Uh...hey! What is this? I mean..."

Tony's jaw tightens. Another one who could fight the power of his gift? How could that be? Maybe he is just tired. "Tell me your name."

The young man's face pales, and the veins in his neck throb visibly as he fights unsuccessfully against Tony's power. "Daniel Gilroy." The words explode in a puff of breath. "Fuck! How are you doing that?"

"Everybody calls him Dandy." Bull shrugs a shoulder, dismissing Danny's glare. "He's got a power, too, boyo. Like us. Might as well tell him what he wants to know. He's gonna find out anyway."

Tony quirks an eyebrow in surprise. "Both of you have gifts?" He stares hard at Dandy. "What's your power?"

"I...aw, fuck! I can get ideas, pictures in me head, when I touch stuff."

He knows then and there that he's just landed two fish for his pet project. Perfect fish, too, and both with gifts! They'd fit like hand-in-glove at the Club, and who knows? Those powers of theirs might turn out to be useful.

He grinned as he watched the two figures walk closer, the wind chilling his teeth. When Anthony Brazzio from Brooklyn, New York made a suggestion, everyone listened and most obeyed without question. It was his gift, the reason he'd been chosen as heir and co-owner of Club Raven. He was very selective about using it, but when he did it never, ever failed to work. Bull and Dandy were two prime examples. He'd told them to come to Baltimore, and here they were, right on schedule.

Tony's gift was the Power of Suggestion, and while it wasn't perhaps the most flamboyant of gifts, it had worked well in his stead since he was a lad. He smirked, remembering the first time he realized he could force people to do his will.

"Antonio, dove stai andando? Venitealla chiesa con me stasera. Si tratta di San Ciro's giorno di festa, e siamo già in ritardo! Padre Giovanni sarà arrabbiato!"

His nine-year old self frowns, and shrugs off his mother's hand. What does he care if he's late to Mass? The last place he wants to go is St. Paul's, and the last person he wants to see is Father Giovanni. When he'd gone last Sunday to serve at Mass, the priest wanted to poke about under Tony's cassock in the sanctuary. Telling his mama and papa won't do any good— they'll never believe his word over the priest's. Now hecan feel panic rising, clawing at his chest, trying to steal the air from his lungs as he tries to figure out a way to get out of going to church.

Just as he begins to feel as if the room is closing in, and darkness begins flickering at the edge of his vision, a peculiar feeling washes over him. He suddenly knows without the slightest doubt that his mama will do exactly as he says, if he orders her with conviction.

Maybe he's gone crazy, but it's worth a try. He takes a deep breath and looks his mama in the eye. "Mama, you don't want me to go. You want me to stay home. I ain't feeling well, see? I got a fever."

His mother looks puzzled for a moment, and then begins to scold him. "Antonio! Cosa stai facendo fuori dal letto? Sei malato. Nessuna chiesa oggi. Tornate a letto!"

"Si, Mama." He'll happily go back to bed as she orders, and while the rest of the family is in church, he'lllay there thinking about what had happened and trying to understand. Somehow, he'd made his mama do as he'd wanted. It's a miracle!

Over the next few weeks, he tries several experiments using his newfound power. For his trouble, he gets an apple from the grocer for free, Tommy Catania gives him a new cat's eye marble, and he is the recipient of a peppermint stick from Mr. Greengott at the apothecary, all because he tells each one they want to give him a present.

Deciding his gift must be God's way of saying sorry for taking Tony's papa, sister, and brother away, and leaving Tony and the rest of his family to rot in Five Points, he promises himself not to use it selfishly...except for one more time.

He remembers Mrs. Nunzio's screams when she sees Father Giovanni run down the street stark naked, pulling on his pecker like he was churning butter, and how the policemen had cursed as they hauled the priest away. Last Tony heard, Father Giovanni was locked up in the Blackwell Lunatic Asylum.

After that, he only uses his gift to help feed the family and pay the rent on their flat, and he makes sure to tithe a percentage of every heist to the church in thanks.

Whistling a merry tune and twirling his walking stick, Tony crossed the street to meet Bull and Dandy, ready to begin the next step of his master plan of turning two rough-cut young men into polished diamonds worthy of the best society had to offer.

Chapter One

S uck harder!"

Bull's cock slipped out of Dandy's mouth with an audible *pop*. "Fuck it all, Bull. Quit giving me orders or I'll bite your prick off."

"Aw, come on, boyo. I'm just horny, is all. Me manners ain't top notch when me cock is in your sweet mouth." Bull ran his fingers through Dandy's soft black curls. "Do me now, yeah?"

Dandy's plump lips parted in a small smile as he reached for Bull's cock. It was short and stout like its owner, but his ass twitched remembering how well it fit in Dandy's hole. *Like a cork in a bottle of fine Irish whiskey,* he thought as he took in Bull's length. His lips pulled hard over the tender flesh, velvety soft and salty-bitter. Pulling it in deep until his nose tickled in Bull's ginger pubes, he let it out as slowly as he dared. His tongue worked the fat head until he tasted precome. *Fuck, it never takes Bull long when he gets his cock sucked.* Dandy snorted softly around Bull's prick. *Oh, no, you don't,boyo. If you come you'll roll over and start snoring. You'll not be cheating me out of mine this time!* He grinned and slapped Bull on the thigh. Standing, he stroked himself, letting the head of his cock brush across Bull's lips.

"You're a tease, Dandy-boy. Look!" He fondled his sac. "You left me balls swollen like a pair of oranges!"

"Bah. Grapes, maybe." Dandy laughed and ducked as Bull swatted at him. "And only for a wee bit. Suck me a while, eh? Come on, do me cock justice with that sweet tongue 'o yours."

There was a smile on Bull's face as he rose from the bed

and pushed Dandy down on the mattress. Bull stole a kiss, hard and demanding, full of tongue and teeth and attitude, before he straddled Dandy's legs, bent over, and drew a warm wet tongue in a slow, lazy line from Dandy's knee to his cock. Dandy's cock strained, and his hands fisted in the sheets as he waited impatiently to feel Bull's mouth on his prick.

Bull's head bobbed over Dandy's groin, his red curls bouncing with the motion. Dandy bit his lip as Bull's wet mouth swallowed his cock, tongue working the shaft. When Bull slipped further south and sucked one of Dandy's balls into his mouth, Dandy groaned aloud and threaded his fingers in Bull's hair. "Fuck!" His body grew as tight as catgut on a fiddle, as he began the sweet spiral toward release.

"Oy! You'll not be cheating me, either!" Bull laughed and rolled to the side, stretching out and spooning up against Dandy's body. His cock rubbed against Dandy's hip like a length of hot silk.

Dandy rolled to his side, and reached to the small bedside table for the small vial of oil. He passed it back to Bull. "Hurry, Bull. I'm needing bad."

"I know, Dandy, love. So am I."

Dandy felt movement on the mattress, then Bull's finger, slick with oil, slipped between Dandy's cheeks. When that greased finger breached his hole, he muttered a soft sigh. "That's it, boyo. Work me hole, make it ready for your pretty cock."

Bull didn't answer, but his finger worked itself deeper into Dandy's ass, before another finger slipped in to join it. It wasn't until Bull had three fingers pushed deep into Dandy's hole that he finally pulled out.

Dandy felt suddenly bereft and empty, the slight burn a reminder of what he was missing, but he knew it wouldn't be for long. Bull was ready; Dandy could feel wetness on his hip where Bull's hard cock prodded him. It wasn't long before he felt the heavy, rounded head push into him.

He arched his back, helping Bull slide in, filling him. Fisting his own cock, he began to work the shaft in time with Bull's thrusts. His balls began to swell, precome wetting his hand. "Fuck, Bull! Faster, boyo! Harder!"

Bull obliged, slamming himself into Dandy with hard, loud slapping sounds. His grunts were erotic, pushing past the last of Dandy's control and setting off his orgasm. He cried out, pumping his fist hard, come spilling over it in thick white rivulets. The smell of sex filled the air.

Behind him, Bull's grunts were growing louder while his thrusts grew erratic. Dandy felt the hot gush of come when Bull came. It filled him, slicking his hole, dripping out over his balls.

"Fuck, Dandy." Bull was out of breath, his voice barely a gruff whisper. "Just...fuck."

Dandy chuckled, and wiped his hand on the fine linen sheet. "We did, and it was good, if I do say so meself." He yelped when Bull slapped him on the ass. "Guess we best get dressed and go downstairs. His Nibs said four o'clock for dinner."

Bull swore. "Since when do we take orders from an Eye-talian like Tony Brazzio?" He sat up, resting his back against the velvet-padded backboard. His cock, fully soft now and pale, rested against his thigh, framed prettily by a thatch of reddish-brown hair. "Look, we need to have a plan, me boy. We came here because Brazzio used his power on us, but we don't have to stay, right?"

"Yeah, but I don't want to go back to Five Points neither, do you?"

"Nah, 'course not. Do I look like a looney? Who would want to go back to picking rags and stealing pennies to live?" Bull scratched his chin, scruffy with two days' worth of growth. "No, see, I see this hereas a new beginning, bucko."

Dandy rolled to his back and laid his head on Bull's shoulder.

"Yeah? So, what's your plan?"

Bull shifted, slipping his arm behind Dandy's head. "What is this place we're at?"

"Here? Club Raven, a hoighty-toighty supper club for them high society folk."

"Them *rich* high society folk." Bull winked at him and kissed his forehead. "Here's what I say. We spend a few days here, scout things out. Pretend we're cleaning up like Brazzio wants, toeing the line. Then, when Brazzio thinks he's got us where he wants us, we relieve those high society farts of their nice fat wallets and run. Go to Chicago, or Boston, maybe. Set ourselves up real nice."

Dandy lifted his head and grinned at him. "Smart lad. So, do we get up and get dressed for supper?"

Bull nodded. "Sunday best behavior, boyo. Don't want Brazzio knowin' what we've got planned."

Dandy popped off the bed and padded to the dresser where a porcelain pitcher and basin waited. Several soft cloths were folded neatly next to the washbasin. He poured water into the basin and picked up the soap, lifting it to his nose. It smelled like flowers, and he smiled. Wetting a cloth, he soaped up and Bull joined him as he started to wash.

By the time they were done, both were pleased with how they looked, and held their heads high as they left the room. They were in great spirits as they approached the main staircase which would take them down to the first floor.

A huge man with skin as dark as ebony stood between them and the stairs. Tony had told them the man's name, but Dandy didn't quite remember it. It was something exotic from deepest Africa, Tony had said. Kwana...Kweena...Kwanele. That was it. Kwanele was a Zulu. Even Dandy and Bull had heard of the Zulus. Fierce warriors, them. Kwanele looked the part, too. He towered over Dandy and Bull by several hands, and his teeth, brilliant white, were sharpened into points. Tony said Kwanele's power was defense, and he was stationed at the top of the stairs to keep the Club Raven residents safe.

Dandy believed it. He would've hated to get on Kwanele's bad side. He nodded and grinned at Kwanele, who stared stoically down at him. Dandy didn't draw a free breath until after they were past the giant with the shark's smile.

If things went south with Bull's plan, Dandy sincerely hoped it wouldn't be Kwanele who came after them.

Chapter Two

Tony sat on a stool in Club Raven's huge kitchen. A plate piled high with fragrant spaghetti Bolognese sat in front of him, accompanied by another dish holding an array of meatballs, sausage, and braciole. He held a tiny saucer full of grated cheese, and drizzled some over the top of the spaghetti with a delicate silver spoon. "Mama, it smells delicious."

A very round woman hovered nearby. She wore a black silk faile mourning dress, and a long white apron. Her only jewelry was a simple gold wedding ring, a broach fashioned from human hair that was pinned to her ample bosom, and a pair of black rosary beads she kept in her apron pocket. Her gray-streaked black hair was neatly braided and pinned into a coronet encircling her head. She flicked her fingers impatiently toward his plate. "*Si, si. Mangiare.*"

Tony chuckled. "*Si, si.* I'm eating, Mama. You're going to make me fat." He twirled his fork in the pasta and lifted it to his mouth. His eyes closed in near ecstasy at his first taste. Nobody cooked like his mama. It was why he brought her to Club Raven as his private chef. She had a nice little apartment behind the kitchen. This way he could see to her needs, and didn't have to worry about her living in Five Points, but she could still feel useful.

"*Perché hai portato quei due ragazzi irlandesi qui?*" She made the forked sign of protection with her fingers. "*Sono problemi.*"

"I know the two Irish boys are trouble." He smiled at her, then speared a piece of sausage on his fork. "I need to make them respectable. *Rispettabile*, you understand?"

"*Stai andando a mettere se stessi in difficoltà, Antonio.*"

"I won't get myself in trouble, Mama. I told you—I'm one of the owners in this place." He shook his head. Mama just couldn't believe that her son, poor little Anthony Brazzio from Five Points, could co-own a magnificent building like Club Raven. It was as if Mama spent her days with one eye always looking for the trouble she was sure was coming. "I admit, though, I'm wondering if maybe I made a mistake bringing them here. They're up to something, I can feel it."

Mama grunted low in her throat, a sound Tony knew well from his childhood. It meant Mama wasn't happy, and a scolding was shortly to follow. He stopped himself from cringing by sheer force of will.

"*Quindi, perché li hai portato qui? Mandarli via!*" Mama waved her hand as if dismissing the whole problem.

"Mama, I've explained this before. You and me, we're not society people, but everyone else here is. I always feel like members of the club look down on me, don't trust me because of where I come from. I think most of them believe I'm an exception to the rule, a curiosity. I want to show them that anyone from places like Five Points can better themselves. That's why I brought those two men here." He sighed, and put his fork down.

Mama smiled, and put a reassuring hand on Tony's shoulder. "*Poi farlo, Antonio. Mostrali.*"

Tony smiled back, and patted her hand. "I will, Mama. I'll do it, and I'll show them all."

He stood up, and bent to place a kiss on Mama's cheek. "*Grazie* for the spaghetti. I'll see you for dinner."

Leaving Mama to the room she was happiest in—the kitchen—he went in search of the other two owners.

He found Julian in the library sitting in one of the leather armchairs, a book open in his hands and a snifter of brandy at his side. Julian's perfectly couffed silvery hair glinted in the lamplight.

Julian spoke without ever lifting his gaze from the page. "I don't know if you'll succeed, but I have no issues with your endeavors. I should think you would wish to finish what you've begun."

Tony's jaw tightened. "Don't do that. I hate it when you read my mind."

"Sorry, my dear boy. It's habit, you know."

"Well, just keep your trap shut until I ask the question next time." Tony's mouth slanted into a sardonic little smile as he applied a bit of his own power to the remark. Julian *would* wait until Tony asked his question next time. Tony had just made sure of it.

Julian finally looked up at him. Tony could practically feel the glare Julian shot across the room. "Did you just use your power on me? You did. How dare you?"

Tony's smile broadened. "Tit for tat, Julian."

Julian sank back into his chair and crossed his legs. "Very well. Let's call it even between us, then, shall we?"

"Sure, sure. We're square. Do you know where Matthias is?"

"I haven't the foggiest notion. I am not his nanny."

Tony rolled his eyes. "Fine. I'll find him on my own."

"You are most welcome."

Tony frowned. "I didn't say thank you."

"I know. I was attempting to point out your dreadful manners."

"*Madre di Dio.*Okay, okay. Thank you." Tony replied, not caring how sarcastic he sounded. He sighed and turned to leave. *What a stuffed shirt.*

"I heard that."

"Stop reading my mind!" He called over his shoulder as he

stalked out of the library.

He wandered in and out of rooms, but Matthias was nowhere to be found on the first floor. Climbing the main staircase, he approached Kwanele, craning his neck to look up at the huge Zulu warrior. "Evening, Kwanele."

Kwanele bared his sharpened teeth in a grim parody of a smile. "*Amakhosi.*"

Tony tried not to smile. He liked being called a chief, especially since he knew it was a term of respect from the very ferocious warrior. All of the owners trusted Kwanele implicitly. He'd never met a more honest, if intimidating, man, and since Kwanele's power was defense, he kept the club owners safe from anyone who might be plotting against them. "Do you happen to know where I can find Matthias?"

Kwanele's large head bobbed once. "In suite with Koni."

His anger at Julian cooled by the time he reached Matthias's door. Raising hishand to knock on the door, he heard noises coming from within. Gasping, groaning, and moaning noises, along with a measured thumping he recognized as a headboard beating against the wall. He quirked an eyebrow. *Well, I guess I know what Matthias and Koni are up to.* He sighed. *I wish I was doing the same. No sense interrupting them—Matthias would only get annoyed, and I'm not in the mood for an argument. If Julian doesn't mind my plan, I doubt Matthias will.* He turned around and went back the way he came.

When he reached Kwanele, he paused again. "Do you happen to know where Bull and Dandy went? I mean, Seamus and Daniel."

Kwanele shook his head. "No, *Amakhosi.* I sense only their plotting, not their thoughts. They think to steal from guests of*Amakhosi.*"His expression stiffened, becoming a cold mask of studied indifference. "*Amakhosi*wish Kwanele to kill these two men?"

Tony's eyes widened. "No, no, Kwanele. That won't be necessary. Thank you for telling me, though. I'll take care of them."

Those stupid idioti*! I brought them here, gave them everything they need to succeed, and this is how they repay me?By stealing from my guests? I don't need Kwanele to do it. I'll kill them myself!*Then he let out a long, low sigh*as* his conscience admonished him for his rash thoughts. *What would you do if you were in their place? The same fucking thing, that's what. You'd try to steal the gold teeth out of the members' mouths if you could, too. Stash the house silver in your luggage along with anything else you could find of value.* He chuckled quietly. *They're just like me. Or, like how I was."* He would take care of things himself, as quietly as possible, and prove to everyone that just because you came from poor beginnings didn't mean you couldn't better yourself.

Tony offered up a tight smile. "Thank you anyway, Kwanele." He trotted down the stairs to the main floor and made his way to the club room, where members gathered to drink fine whiskey and brandy and smoke cigars. Perhaps he'd find Bull and Dandy there, or maybe some of the members had seen them. Given their manners and attitudes, they were sure to stick out among the cultured members of Club Raven. He only hoped Bull and Dandy hadn't stripped the members of everything but their underwear already.

The club room was nearly empty. Not surprising—it was nearing supper hour, and the dining room would soon open for those members who weren't going home for dinner. He looked around, his gaze settling on a plump, older gentleman sporting a luxurious Imperial mustache, seated in an armchair near the fireplace. He searched his memory for a name. It took a moment before it came to him.

Lord Winston Thurgood, owner of Thurgood Shipping. He'd brought his family fortune with him from England along with his title, a wife, and several children. Lord Thurgood was one of their "special" members who had access to the otherwise off-limits rooms in Club Raven. He liked to be disciplined as a naughty schoolboy, Tony remembered, smirking, and then fucked until he limped.

"Good afternoon, Lord Thurgood." He gave Thurgood a short bow and a smile. "I trust you're enjoying the fire and your cigar?"

Thurgood peered at him, no doubt also trying to come up with a name. "Angelo, is it? No, that isn't right. Giuseppe? Some Italian name, yes?"

He bit back a retort. "Yes. It's Tony, sir. Short for Anthony."

"Ah, yes. Right, right. That's it, of course." Thurgood plugged a fat cigar between his teeth and puffed. Blue smoke wavered around his head like a dying halo. "Jolly good."

"I was wondering if perhaps you'd seen two young men in here earlier. One is slender and dark, the other is a redhead and stocky. Irish, the both of them."

Thurgood seemed to mull it over, rolling his cigar from one side of his mouth to the other. "Yes, now that I think of it, I believe they were in here a while ago. Caused quite a commotion, I'd say. Something about missing billfolds."

Tony ground his teeth. *Those stupid bastards! I'm going to wring their Irish necks when I get hold of them.* "And your billfold, Sir Thurgood? Is it safe and sound?"

"Mine? Why, my dear boy, no one could possibly steal my billfold. I keep it right here, next to my heart..." Thurgood's hand patted his jacket. "That's odd. I always keep it right here." He patted the other side of his jacket, then his checked his vest. "It can't be! How could...?" He glared up at Tony. "I demand, sir, a full explanation and return of my billfold immediately!" Thurgood huffed, ruffling his carefully waxed mustache.

Tony took a deep, steadying breath. He could worry about Bull and Dandy later. Right now, he needed to address the situation at hand. He locked gazes with Thurgood, and gave a little "push" with his talent. "Never fear. We'll messenger your billfold to your home, Sir Thurgood. You aren't angry."

"Of course I'm angry!" Thurgood's face was turning an interesting shade of purple.

Tony turned his power up a notch. "No, you aren't."

"I...I'm not?"

"No. You're quite content. You're going to go into the dining room and have supper—compliments of the club, of course— then you're going to go home. In fact, when you get home you'll have forgotten your billfold was stolen. You won't know what happened to it."

"Of course, I'll have no idea. Must've misplaced it, is that it? Of course. How very absentminded of me." Thurgood blinked, and stubbed out his cigar. "Dear boy, you must excuse me. I'm suddenly very hungry."

"Please, be my guest tonight in the dining room. Let me walk you in."

"Very kind, Angelo. Indeed."

"My name is Anthony, Sir Thurgood. Tony, remember?"

"Ah, so it is. So it is."

As Tony offered his elbow to the elderly Thurgood and escorted him to the dining room, he silently stewed. Bull and Dandy were definitely turning out to be more trouble than they were worth, but he was going to set things right if it was the last thing he did.

Chapter Three

Bull's biceps bulged and his back ached as he lugged the heavy valise through the alley. He could feel the strain all the way up into his neck, but smiled against the pain. It would be worth it. They had a bloody fortune socked away between the suitcase and the pillowcase Dandy carried.

What a haul!Best of all, they'd gotten it without barely breaking a sweat. Those old fucks at the club were as stupid as they were stuffy. He and Dandy picked a dozen pockets clean of billfolds, along with two gold pocket watches and a pair of diamond cufflinks. Added to the silk damask napkins, crystal vases, sterling silver cutlery, candlesticks, coffee pots, gravy boats, and soup tureens they'd lifted from the buffets in the dining room before it opened for dinner, and they could live like kings for a month or more once they hocked everything.

They'd paused only once since leaving the club, and that was to relieve the billfolds of their currency, stuffing the money into their own pockets.

"How much do you think we got, Bull?" Dandy's voice called to him, sounding as winded as Bull felt. He had the pillowcase thrown over one shoulder, and his back bowed from the weight of it.

"A little over a hunnert in cash money, but with the rest? Dunno, but it's a tidy sum, yeah?"

"Enough to keep us in food, whiskey, and ass for a good long while, I'll bet."

"Providing we find someone willing to buy it all and not ask too many questions about where we got it." He paused to catch his breath, setting the heavy valise down. He sat on it to rest for a minute or two. "Best we head toward the wharfs. There's bound to be pawnshops over there what won't be too interested in where the goods they buy come from, yeah?"

Dandy nodded. "Where should we go after we shed ourselves of this stuff? I admit to ya I ain't too keen to go back to Five Points."

"Me, neither, boyo. Ain't nothing back there for us. For the time being, I figure we'll ask about for a bawdy house. No gentleman from Club Raven would set foot in one of them, I'm thinking. We can sit pretty there while we make plans on where to go next."

"Good idea. Hey! Maybe we should think about starting our own house, Bull. But for men like us, see? No women allowed. We could decorate it nice, hire on some good-looking nancies…"

Bull whistled softly through his teeth. "That'd take more than we got here, boyo. Starting a business is expensive. There's property to rent or buy, whores to hire, furniture, food, not to mention palms to grease. Best we think on it more." He stood up, lifted the suitcase, and started walking again. "Which way to the wharf do you ken?"

Dandy paused, and shifted the weight of his pillowcase to his other shoulder. He pointed to the left. "That way, I think."

"All right then, let's be off with us."

They walked for a dozen or more blocks, careful to keep to the shadows in case someone from the club was hunting them, before catching even a whiff of the sea in the air. By the time they reached the wharfs, they were both feeling irritable, hungry, and tired, and a wee bit regretful for having run from the comforts of Club Raven.

"There, Bull. See it? The sign?" Dandy pointed toward a wooden depiction of three hanging balls, the widely understood symbol of a pawnbroker.

Bull nodded, and they stepped up their pace, eager to ease down their burdens and collect on the stolen goods.

The store was dimly lit by a few strategically hung lanterns, and was filled with shelves jumbled with piles of pottery, music boxes, porcelain statues, dresses, coats, and shoes. The proprietor sat at the rear of the store behind a long wooden counter stacked high with more offerings. He nodded at Bull and Dandy as they threaded their way through the cramped room toward him.

"Help you?"

Bull laid the valise on the counter in front of the pawnbroker and opened it. The silver piled insideglinted dully under the yellow lamplight. Dandy dumped the contents of his pillowcase next to it, making an impressive pile of silver and crystal. "How much for all of this?"

The shopkeeper—an older man with a wispy beard, thick gray eyebrows, and fish lips—frowned, ghosting his fingers over the merchandise. He picked up a butter knife and examined it, reading the elegantly engraved initials. "C.R. Where'd you lift this from?"

Bull frowned and took the knife from the man's hand, depositing it back in the valise. "Where we got it is none of your concern, is it? For all you know my name is Carl Ray. Or Curtis Right." He chuckled at his own wit and elbowed Dandy. "How much?"

The man huffed, blowing air through his thick lips. "A hundred for the lot."

Dandy scoffed at the price. "What! Aw, you're daft. A hunnert dollars for all this? This is quality merchandise. It's the finest silver, me bucko, and those be real diamonds set in gold!"

"And the pocket watches! Don't forget those." Bull pushed one toward the shopkeeper. "Solid gold."

The proprietor carefully opened one and chuckled. "And

inscribed, you great lunk. 'To my darling Edward, from your loving Cecilia.' I suppose I'd be correct if I guessed neither of your Christian names might be Edward or that either of you know anyone named Cecilia?"

"Bah, what you do care? It's gold. Melt 'em down."

"Do I look like a smelting works to you? No, no. A hundred for the lot, no more, and you're lucky I'm offering that much and not calling for the constable."

Dandy started to scoop the silver back into the pillowcase. "Fine, ye tightfisted bastard. We'll take our goods somewhere else, is all."

The shopkeeper smiled, showing a set of snaggled, yellowed teeth. "Fine, fine. Go on. Of course, there ain't another pawnbroker on the wharf except for Jauncy's, and he's a thief if ever there was one. But you go ahead, take your goods over there. Just so you know, though, my price goes down to fifty dollars the minute you step outside of this shop."

Bull swore, and slammed a hand down on the counter. "Thievery! One-fifty, then, for it all."

The proprietor smirked at them. "One hundred, and not a penny more."

Bull and Dandy exchanged a glance. It was brief, but a wealth of information passed unspoken between them. Furrowing his brow, Bull growled at the shopkeeper. "Fine. A hundred."

Dandy watched closely as the man went to a brass register which sat off to one side, and pressed a key. The tray popped open, and he took several bills from it.

"One hundred." He counted out the bills into Bull's hand. "Have a good evening, lads."

Bull sniffed at him, and shoved the bills deep into his pocket. "Oh, we will, we will. Come on, Dandy. Let's go."

Outside, Bull reached into his coat pocket and pulled out a large wad of cash he'd spirited out of the register drawer with his power.

Dandy grinned at him. "When do you suppose he'll notice he was robbed?"

Bull shrugged. "Don't know. We'll be far gone by then. Besides, it was his own fuckingfault for trying to cheat us, eh?"

They'd walked a block or so when Bull stopped and pointed to a tavern on the corner. "Let's stop for a pint and toast our good fortune, yeah?"

Dandy nodded, and followed Bull into the establishment. It was more brightly lit than the pawnshop, but not by much. They took seats at the long counter, where the barkeep served them two dark ales in cheap tin mugs. "Do you happen to know a place a man can go to...er, take care of certain needs, boyo?"

One of the bartender's eyebrows arched over his eye. "What sort of needs are we talking about?"

"You know. Like the kind of itch a man gets now and then."

Dandy looked over his shoulder, then leaned in closer to the barkeep. "The kind a woman can't scratch."

The bartender sniffed, and didn't bother trying to hide the look of disgust on his face. "Aw, you two are a pair, ain't you? What makes you think I know anything about places like that? I'm a God-fearing Christian soul, got a wife and five children, and I don't—"

Bull slid several shiny coins across the counter, which quickly disappeared into the barkeep's apron pocket.

"Maude Breem has a place on Lancaster. The Soiled Dove, it's called. Maude's clients are a...peculiar bunch. She serves all types and wants over there."

"Does she have rooms to let?"

"I suppose so. If not, there are a few hotels near there, too. The Arlington is good, and includes midnight lunches with the price."

"Much obliged, bucko." Bull downed the last of his ale, and left with Dandy following close behind.

They swallowed laughter and hurried their step when, in the distance, they heard the pawnbroker shouting for the constable because he'd been robbed.

The Soiled Dove was a three-story brick building on Lancaster Street. It sat sandwiched between two structures identical to itself, distinguished only by a discreet sign bearing its name hung next to the front door. Bull and Dandy climbed the few stairs to the stoop, and rapped the lion's head knocker sharply against the wooden door.

A Negrowith graying hair, clad in a dark servant's uniform and crisp white gloves, answered the door. He gave them a courtly bow. "Welcome, gentlemen. Please come in. Miss Breem be accepting guests in the front parlor."

They exchanged a surprised look, then lifted their chins and straightened their spines, and followed the butler into the house.

That the house wasn't an ordinary residence was immediately apparent, even to Bull and Dandy, who weren't the most sophisticated men in town and freely admitted to it. Oil paintings in ornate, gilded frames hung on the damask-covered walls. Tall, sparkling crystal vases held sprays of brilliantly colored flowers. Daintily tatted lace doilies protected the highly-polished surfaces of dark, well-oiled furniture. Plush sofas and elegant chairs, both covered in rich, ruby velvet,were placed around the parlor and clustered in front of a large fireplace where a cheery fire crackled.

The parlor was empty except for one person, a woman dressed in a pale blue satin and lace tea gown. Her gray hair was swept up in a sleek chignon, and she sat with the posture of a queen on an intricately carved and deeply cushioned Rococo Revival-style chair. She smiled at them, and waved them to seats on a settee across from her.

"Welcome, my dears. My name is Maude Breem, proprietress of this fine establishment. Please, sit down. May I offer you refreshment?" She gestured toward the elderly servant. "Jacques, serve the gentlemen each a glass of that luscious D'Oliveiras Malvasia Reserva." She turned back to Bull and Dandy. "A lovely, sweet wine. A gift from a very satisfied client." She smiled, and settled back against her chair.

Bull cleared his throat. "Um, we were wondering—"

Maude held up a hand, effectively silencing him. "Oh, shh, dear. One should never discuss business before the societal niceties are exchanged. It's gauche."

Bull muttered an apology and sat back, feeling his cheeks heat up. He felt like he'd been admonished by one of the nuns back at St. Vincent's School for Boys where he'd attended until he was nine. This woman reminded him of the nuns—her haughty posture, her condescending manner. His knuckles and back still bore the scars of the nuns' attempts to beat the devil out of him.

He'd *hated* those nuns with his entire being, and that did very little to endear Maude Breem to him. Still, he kept quiet, swallowing the insults dancing on the tip of his tongue. Who did this glorified whore think she was, shushing him like a child?

The butler returned, carrying a gleaming silver tray on which three crystal glasses and a bottle of wine balanced, distracting Bull from his thoughts. He accepted a glass of freshly poured wine and glanced at Dandy, wondering if he should drink or wait for Maude to sip hers first.

"Drink up, boys. Enjoy!" Maude tilted the glass to her lips. Bull noticed the wine was almost the same color as Maude's lips—deep, dark, ruby red.

The wine was very sweet, and pungent. Bull never cared much for wine—he enjoyed a nice dark ale far more, and considered wine a sissy's drink—but he drank it anyway, downing it like medicine. The butler took his empty glass and left the room. "So, can we talk business now?"

She smiled at him. "Very well. What can I do for you two gentlemen?"

Dandy leaned in, his almost full glass held in both hands. "We need a room, yeah?"

Maude sipped her wine. "We're not in the business of letting out rooms, dear."

Bull dug in his pocket and pulled out the bills he got from the pawnbroker. "You sure about that, love?"

With a smile that pressed her lips into a dark red slash, Maude cocked an eyebrow. "I didn't say we never did it. I simply said it isn't our business." She took another sip. "You know, I could use a couple of boys like you two. I've got clients who would pay a great deal for a few hours with a pair of fresh-faced Irish lads." She leaned forward. "I pay well, and I treat my boys like my own sons."

Bull sputtered. "Do we look like whores to you?"

Maude's gaze hardened. "Perhaps we have no business to discuss after all. You're a rude young man."

Dandy punched Bull in the shoulder. "Please, ma'am, he's sorry. His temper runs away with him sometimes, yeah? He don't mean anything by it."

"Oh?" Maude looked hard at Bull, then smiled. "We all make mistakes from time to time, I suppose. I certainly meant no insult. I hold my boys in the highest regard, and don't make the offer for employment lightly."

Bull hung his head in a look of shame he didn't feel. "Dandy is right. Me temper will be the ruin of me, Missus."

"Think nothing of it. Apology accepted, dear boy. I hope you understand I meant no insult in the offering." Maude picked up a tiny golden bell from the table at her side and rang it. Jacques appeared almost immediately. "Jacques, have Missy make up one of the guest rooms on the third floor with fresh linens, and tell Maurice we'll have two additional diners at meals."

"Yes'm." Jacques bowed and left again.

Maude returned an inscrutable gaze to the boys. When she spoke again, Bull nearly tumbled off his seat at the sound of her thick brogue. "All right, then, boyos. Don't sell me a dog. Tell me why you need a room here. Who's after ye?"

Bull looked at Dandy and saw the same surprise in his eyes that Bull felt. "You're from the old country?"

She laughed with a much heartier sound than either of them would've credited her with having. She looked like her laugh would be dainty and delicate, like fine crystal, but instead it was deep and loud, and as sturdy as a shillelagh. "Born and bred in County Cork, brought over by me first husband, Matthew Kelly, God rest his soul. He died shortly after we made port in New York, left me penniless. Still had me looks, thank God, and I met and married Connor Breem soon after. He brought me down here, to Baltimore."

Bull and Dandy were silent, caught up in her story. They watched as she drained the rest of her wine. "What happened to him, Missus? Your second husband?"

She sighed, her smile fading until it looked small and sad. "He died as well. Influenza. I loved him, you know, me Connor. He was a good man, but had a poor head for figures. He left me only a small sum and I decided then and there not to leave me future in any man's hands ever again." She found her smile again, and although it wreathed them with wrinkles, her blue eyes sparkled. "So, I took the few dollars he bequeathed me and parlayed it into this thrivin' establishment. Started with just two boys. Now I've got me fifteen boys, and me clients come from near and far to sample me wares. Rich men think having a brogue means you're stupid, so I worked hard to lose me Irish lilt." She leaned forward, and lowered her voice to a whisper. "Now, you know all about me, so tell me true, boyos...who's hunting you?"

Dandy and Bull exchanged a look, and Dandy gave Bull a small nod. "Go on, Bull. Tell her."

"Well, Dandy and me, we lived in Five Points up in Manhattan. We ran a good game, kept ourselves in clover, mostly. But this Eye-talian guy, Tony, he comes and offers to bring us to Baltimore, to this place called Club Raven—"

Maude's eyes widened. "Club Raven? Sure an' I've heard stories about that place! Tell me everything."

"Well, Missus, we didn't really see much. We didn't stay there long."

Maude laughed. "I suppose you left with your pockets a mite heavier than they were goin' in, eh, boyos?"

They grinned at her, and Bull suddenly felt more at home than he had since leaving Five Points. He found his former flash of anger dissolving. Maude was good people, Bull decided. More than good—she was Irish, from the old country, and knew what living a hardscrabble life was like. Didn't she pull herself up by the bootstraps after two husbands went toes up on her, leavingher without a pot to piss in? Couldn't have been easy for her, but she did it.

"So, I suppose the gent...what was his name? Tommy?"

"Tony, Missus." Dandy offered the correction with a shy smile. "Tony Brazzio."

"Ah, so it is. Tony. I suppose he's looking for you and whatever you stole?"

"Seems likely. That's why we come here. We pawned everything, and figured no highfalutin' stuffed shirt from Club Raven would come to a bawdy house, so nobody would see us. Give us some time to make plans, you see."

Maude laughed again. "And that shows just how smart you

are, boyo—or aren't, I should say. I get lots of well-heeled gents in this place. The mayor even comes in now and then." She held up a hand before either of them could speak. "But don't worry. We Irish take care of our own. You can have a room upstairs until you decide what you want to do. Everyone who comes in here knows to keep their mouths shut about what and who they see inside these walls, or they'll never be welcome back again." She leaned forward. "And just remember, me offer still stands if you want to work for me."

"Yes, Missus. Thank you." Bull smiled, not getting angry this time. How could he? It was obvious now Maude meant no offense.

Dandy nodded and offered his thanks as well. "We'll always remember your kindness, Missus."

She lifted the bell and rang it again. By the time Jacques returned to the room, her voice had returned to the cultured tones she'd been using when Bull and Dandy first arrived. "Escort these fine gentlemen upstairs, Jacques. They'll be our guests for a time, and they're certain to want to rest before dinner." She nodded to Bull and Dandy. "Go with Jacques, and he'll see you settled in. Dinner is served at seven. I'll have someone bring in appropriate attire for you. Oh, and I'm hosting a private event tonight. A party of sorts. You gentlemen are welcome to attend."

Bull exchanged a curious glance with Dandy. Whatever this event was, it sounded a lot more exciting to Bull than sitting in a room staring at the ceiling all night. "We'll be there, Missus."

Her smile as they left her made Bull wonder what she knew that they didn't.

Chapter Four

Dinner was delicious, generous slices of rare roast beef served with pearl onions, green beans, and boiled potatoes. Bull and Dandy ate until they thought they might burst. It was a lesson learned early in Five Points—eat well when food was in front of you because you could never be sure if you'd go hungry tomorrow.

To her credit, Maude didn't comment on either their piggery or lack of manners. Instead, she nibbled at her own plate, and sampled more of the rich, red wine she'd served them earlier, patiently waiting until they were through.

"Oh, and that was good grub." Dandy wiped his mouth with a square of fine linen. "Best I've had in a good long while."

Maude sat back and allowed the maid to remove her dish. "Didn't they feed you well at Club Raven? I've heard their food is excellent."

Bull shrugged. "It was okay if you like fancy Eye-talian food, but it wasn't good, old fashioned Irish meat and potatoes like you got here."

"Ah, I am quite fond of Italian cuisine. There is a lovely restaurant on the other side of town that serves the most delectable chicken scampi. I've been told their chef studied in both Italy and France."

Dandy blinked. "They got schools for *cooks* in those places?" He turned to Bull. "Imagine that, wasting time going to school to learn how to boil a potato! Me ma never went to school, and she could cook just fine."

"Yeah, when your Pa wasn't whaling on her."

Dandy nodded, and pushed his plate away. It was as clean as if it'd been washed. "Like I said, this was good, though."

Jacques had been standing behind and just to the right of Maude, quietly attentive to her every need, almost invisible unless she called on him. Now he moved to help her rise from her chair. "I do hope you plan to attend my little soirée this evening, gentlemen. I'm certain you'll enjoy yourselves immensely."

"Yes, ma'am, we'll be there." Bull nodded, and then picked at the borrowed evening suit he wore. It was better than any suit he'd ever worn, better even than the clothes Tony bought for him and Dandy at Club Raven, but was a little big for him. "Do we need to wear these duds for this party?"

For some reason, she thought that was amusing, and chuckled. Even Jacques smirked as he moved her chair back to allow her to rise. "Oh, all the clothing you require is waiting for you in your room. The party will begin promptly at eight o'clock. I will welcome my guests downstairs in the parlor, and then progress up to the ballroom and adjacent rooms on the second floor. You may join us in the ballroom. I hope to see you then, my dears." She left, with Jacques following dutifully behind her.

"What do you suppose sort of party this is going to be?" Dandy tugged on his detachable collar, digging a finger between the stiff celluloid material and his skin.

Bull snorted. "What sort of party do you ken goes on in a bawdy house, Dandy? The kind that leaves a man with a soft dick and an empty wallet, that's what."

"Oh!" He grinned. "Are you thinking what I'm thinking?"

"That there'll be billfolds aplenty ripe for the plucking?"

Dandy frowned at him. "Aw, now, we oughtn't be stealing from Maude's guests, Bull. She's been good to us, she has, and she's from the old country."

"Exactly! She's one of us—I'd bet she'd steal the milk from a new mother's bosom if she thought she could sell it. She won't mind if we help ourselves to a bit of scratch if the opportunity arises, boyo."

Dandy seemed to think about it, then grinned at Bull. "Well, then, what's say we go get cleaned up a bit before the party starts? After all, we want to look our best when that opportunity comes knocking at our door, don't we?"

"Indeed we do!" Bull stood, scraping his chair back. He bowed deeply, and swept his arm in a grand gesture. "After you, my dear Mr. Gilroy."

"Oh, no, after you."

"No, no. I insist."

Dandy gave a short, sharp nod, and tilted his nose up in the air. "Then I don't mind if I do, Mr. O'Brian."

Bull followed Dandy from the dining room, retracing their original steps to the room they shared. They noticed fresh water and towels for washing were set on the bureau, but the only items of clothing they saw were two simple black masks laid on the bed.

"I thought Maude said she was gonna send clothes for us to wear. What's the masks for?" Dandy fingered one of them. It was fashioned from the same material as his collar, and long silken cords had been attached to each side of the mask to be tied behind the head. "We gonna rob banks tonight or something?"

Bull rolled his eyes. "Aw, you're a real dimwit sometimes, Dandy. There *ain't* no clothes...except for the masks. Get it? These are so nobody recognizes anybody else at the party."

Dandy's lips curved in a wide smile. "Oh, I get it! Sounds like fun, Bull."

"Bah. We're not going there to have fun. We're going to work."

"Yeah, but Bull, if nobody's got no clothes on, where are the marks gonna put their wallets? And where are we going to stash the money we steal?"

Bull blinked in confusion. "I...we...well, I don't know, right off. We'll figure it out later. Come on, let's get washed up and dressed. Or undress. You know what I mean. I don't want to be late."

They felt a little uncomfortable and exposed as they walked down the stairs to the second floor where the ballroom was located, keeping their hands cupped over their privates. Naked while together in the privacy of their room or even in one of the dark alleys back in Five Points was one thing, but prancing around in the well-lit halls of Maude Breem'sbawdy house with their dangly bits flopping about for all and sundry to see was something else entirely.

All they wore were the black masks Maude had provided, and somehow wearing that small bit of fabric over his eyes made Bull feel even more naked than if he'd worn nothing at all. Bull's face burned, and he knew his cheeks were as red as his hair, although he noticed the chambermaids and other servants averted their eyes as they passed with what looked like practiced ease. He supposed seeing naked men running around the house was nothing new to them, but it didn't make him feel any more at ease.

When they reached the ballroom, the gilded double doors were open. The room was huge, taking up one entire side of the second floor. Inside, instead of the elegantly set tables they expected, they found numerous feather mattresses strewn on the floor, draped with black silk and satin fabric. Small tables were set between them, each holding bottles of oil and a few strange doodads like strings of large beads and carvings that looked suspiciously like penises.

"What do you expect those are for, Bull?" Dandy pointed to a large object easily nine inches in length and three inches wide, carved from darkly oiled wood.

"I expect it gets shoved up someone's ass," Bull replied. "Looks like a dick, don't it, and as far as I know, that's what a fella does with his cock in a place like this."

"Why use something like that? Is it for folks who don't have a dick of their own? Like them men we heard tell about who got shot up in Lincoln's War?"

"I don't know. Maybe, maybe not. These rich folk are just plain odd, boyo."

"Guess we'll find out, huh?"

"*You* find out. Ain't nobody fucking *my* ass with no wooden cock."

Dandy huffed at him. "Did I say I wanted to shove one of them things up my ass?"

"You didn't say you didn't."

"Aw, Bull, now—"

Bull cut him off with a nudge from his elbow. "I'm just kidding, boyo. Relax, yeah?"

An intricately carved mahogany screen partitioned off one corner of the room. Musicians must've been set up behind it, because Bull and Dandy could hear them tuning up. Soon music began to play, although it was something without words, some classical piece that neither Bull nor Dandy recognized. They favored more rollicking songs like *Old Folks at Home* or *Camptown Races*, anyway.

A door on the opposite side of the room opened, and fifteen men filed quietly into the room. All were young and handsome with beautifully sculpted bodies, and all were completely naked. Not one looked the slightest bit embarrassed, even though none of them wore masks. Each of them smiled coquettishly at Bull and Dandy as they spread out across the large room, each one lowering himself onto a mattress and striking a pose that Dandy and Bull instantly saw as seductive.

These are Maude's boys, then, Bull thought, *the whores who work for her.* They all looked at ease and comfortable well fed and well cared for, and not one of them looked unhappy. Indeed, from the way their cocks began to stiffen, they all seemed to be looking forward to the night's festivities.

One young man poured oil onto his fingers from one of the small bottles, then knelt on the mattress, supporting himself with one arm. He reached between his legs and began working his slicked digits into his asshole, slicking the pink flesh. Before long, he had two fingers inserted into his body, sliding them in and out, riding them as his balls swung heavily between his legs.

Most of the others reclined, lazily stroking their cocks into fullness. Watching them brought a likewise reaction from Bull's dick, and it struggled to rise behind his cupped hands.

"Best if you go inside, gent'men. Ma'am's guests be arriving soon." They looked to see a manservant standing next to the doors, shooing them into the room. He wore a neat black uniform tail coat, the white of his starched shirt stark against his dark skin. "You'll find most ever'thing you need inside. Anything else you want, just ask and one of the boys will run for it."

Dandy cleared his throat. "Will Mrs. Breem be coming?"

The manservant chuckled. "Oh, no, sir. This ain't no place for Mrs. Breem. Men only, sir."

Dandy and Bull nodded, and then slipped into the room.

Chapter Five

Keeping their rear ends to the wall, Bull and Dandy left a wide berth betweenthemselves and the mattresses where the fairies lay masturbating or finger fucking themselves.

Bull nudged Dandy. "See anything?"

"Yeah. Lots of dicks and pretty asses. Look at that one over there. That's a tasty morsel, yeah?"

"Not the men, you idiot. Do you see anything worth stealing?"

"Not yet, unless you really want a bottle of oil."

Just then the rumbling of masculine voices could be heard. They turned to see a large group of naked men entering the ballroom. Few were as well-built as the prostitutes. Most of the men were older, for one thing, their graying hair and beards, and rounded potbellies, dead giveaways to their age. They chatted amongst themselves as if well-acquainted, even though they all wore the masks that were supposed to provide anonymity.

"Bull, look. It's like I told you. They ain't got no billfolds on 'em."

Bull swore softly. "Guess we're not lifting anything tonight. A big waste of time, is what this is."

"Don't have to be."

Bull turned to look at Dandy. "What do you mean?"

Dandy lifted a shoulder. "We could have us some fun, can't we? I mean, since plying our trade ain't in the cards for us tonight."

"What? You want to fuck one of them old geezers?"

"No, but I wouldn't mind a turn at that lovely ass over there." Dandy pointed his chin toward one of the prostitutes. "What about you and me having a go at him?"

The man Dandy gestured toward was the one who'd been fingering himself. His ass was full and nicely rounded, his pink hole made even more inviting by the slick fingers sliding in and out of it.

Bull grinned and stroked himself. "I don't think I'd mind that a bit, me boyo. Why, it wouldn't be a hardship at all."

The older men were circulating the room, the first ones in picking out whichever prostitute caught their fancy. Dandy observed that some already had their dicks beings sucked. "Geezers don't waste no time, yeah?"

"Some of them don't look like they have much time left to spare," Bull said, and chuckled. "Move quick now, before somebody else takes him." Stepping lively, he threaded his way between the rows until he reached the mattress where their chosen geycat knelt.

The young man looked up at them from over his shoulder and offered a knowing smile. He continued to finger himself; the sound of his digits sliding into his well-greased ass was wet and inviting. He withdrew his fingers when it became obvious Bull and Dandy were interested in him.

Bull's lips tilted in a knowing smile. "Got a name, boyo?"

"Philippe, *monsieur.*" His accent was French, and his voice pleasant as he spoke softly through plump, pink lips. "I am yours for the evening, if you desire, courtesy of Madame Breem."

"Oh, we desire, bucko." Bull gave Philippe's ass a sharp spank, drawing a gasp from Philippe, then gave it a good squeeze. "We desire this ass."

"It is yours." Philippesaid and offered Bull the small bottle of lubricant.

"Wait a minute." Dandy cut in, stroking himself into a full, proud erection. "I'm not wanting to just jump in and fuck. I want that pretty mouth of yours first, Phil."

"Please, it is Philippe, *monsieur*. I would be happy to suck your pretty cock."

"Ooh, listen to the fancy boy. Okay, Fill-eep." Dandy moved closer, brushing the head of his thick cock over Philippe's cheek. "Suck me."

"Me, too. I'm not gonna just stand here and watch, jerking my own cock." Bull nudged Dandy over a bit, touching the tip of his dick to the other side of Phillipe's face. His cock left a wet spot on Philippe's cheek.

Philippe didn't seem the slightest bit concerned about servicing two men at the same time. He rose to his knees and wrapped a hand around each of their cocks, but his mouth went to work on Dandy's first. Without preamble, he swallowed Dandy's length, sucking hard, making loud, juicy noises as he did so.

"Oh, that's pretty. Suck him," Bull said. He reached over and squeezed one of Dandy's butt cheeks, slipping a couple of fingers into the crack.

"Fuck!" Dandy pumped his hips, alternately feeding Philippe his cock and backing against Bull's fingers. "Saints preserve us, his mouth is fucking sweet!" He moaned, and threaded his fingers into Philippe's hair, twisting the strands between them.

"Me now!" Bull growled. He pushed the head of his cock against Philippe's lips, brushing against Dandy's shaft.

Philippe made a contented noise deep in his throat as he let Dandy go and took Bull's cock into his mouth.

Bull's eyes flashed open wide, then rolled to the back of his head with pleasure when Philippe began to hum around his cock. The vibrations travelled to his balls, the sensation unlike anything he'd ever felt before. Feeling a deep need to share the hunger building within him, he turned and pulled Dandy into a deep kiss. Their teeth clashed and tongues danced even as Philippe's mouth worked its magic on his cock.

Dandy finally broke the kiss, panting hard as if out of breath. "I want to fuck him, Bull. I want in that sweet round ass of his."

Bull nodded, too caught up in the lashing Philippe's tongue was giving his cock to argue. From under heavy-lidded eyes he watched Dandy move behind Philippe and pour oil over Philippe's ass crack, then work it in with two fingers.

"Oh, sweet Jesus, his hole is tight. Fucking tight, fucking pretty ass." Dandy removed his fingers, then used them to spread Philippe's ass cheeks. Bull smiled as he watched Dandy's cock slip inside Philippe's body.

They shared Philippe, finding a rhythm that worked for all three of them. Dandy would thrust into Philippe from behind while Bull pushed forward. They rode him from opposite ends, grunting and groaning with lusty pleasure, unaware their moans had drawn a crowd of onlookers.

At Maude Breem's parties, the early bird caught the worm— or willing asshole. There were always too many guests for the prostitutes to accommodate on the first go-round, and many men were left to watch the festivities as they waited their turns. Bull and Dandy were putting on such a lusty, noisy show that they attracted the eyes of most of the guests who hadn't been quick enough to secure a mattress for themselves, or who weren't interested in sharing a man with someone else.

Bull felt his orgasm building, and he pulled out of Philippe's mouth in time to paint Philippe's face with hot streaks of cream.

Across from him Dandy thrusts grew erratic as he came, his head thrown back, veins popping in his neck, his mouth open in a wordless cry.

Only when they'd both emptied their balls on or in Philippe did they realize they had an audience. Neither one was sure what to do, and stood over Philippe, hesitant to move. Bull felt especially unnerved. Should they thank Philippe or just walk away?

"Good show, boys. Move along now and let someone else have a go." A gruff, middle aged man with a bushy beard motioned for them to step away from Philippe. "Got to say, you were pretty to watch."

Another man who'd been watching nodded in agreement. He was rotund, his belly hanging so low over his cock it was nearly invisible. He snapped his fingers, and a manservant appeared almost immediately. "Tell Mrs. Breem I'll pay top dollar for these two, the redhead and the dark-haired one."

Bull narrowed his eyes at the man. "We ain't for sale. We're guests here, same as you."

The man looked surprised, but covered it quickly with a scowl. "Young man, I know everyone who is anyone in Baltimore, but I've never seen you two before. How is it you came to be guests of Mrs. Breem? Where do you come from? Your speech is rough and uneducated. You're obviously of a much lower class than is accepted at this establishment. Naturally I assumed you were geycats."

Dandy snarled at him. "None of your damn business is where we come from." He jerked a thumb at the man. "Did you hear this fat bastard, Bull? He called us low class." He reached out and grabbed the man's arm. "I ought to..."

His voice trailed off and his eyes clouded over for a moment. Bull recognized the look, and realized Dandy's power was at work.

Dandy blinked and let the man go. "Excuse us, sir. We'll be off now. Come on, Bull."

Bull let Dandy pull him away, leaving the man sputtering with indignation. He kept his mouth shut until they were out of the ballroom and nearly to the room they shared upstairs. "What the fuck, boyo? I wanted to slug that fat bastard in the mouth for what he was saying."

"He's the mayor, Bull."

"He's what?"

"The mayor of Baltimore. I saw it when I grabbed him."

"So? That means he can say what he wants about the likes of us? I was having a good time up until then. Then again, a good brawl might've capped off the night."

"No. Think about it, Bull. The mayor of Baltimore is in a bawdy house, watching men fuck each other. What do you think we could do with information like that?"

Understanding came to Bull like a lightning bolt, and he grinned. "Make more money at one time than we could picking a hunnert pockets, I should think!"

Dandy gave a vigorous nod. "And you'd be right, boyo! We'll wait, then go pay the good mayor a visit in his office tomorrow. He just might be interested in making a nice, fat donation to the Dandy and Bull Relief Fund when he finds out what we know about him."

"Right you are! Why, we'll be swimming in money." A thought occurred to him, and he frowned. "But how do we prove it? It'd be our word against his, and he's a big muckety-muck, being mayor and all. Nobody would believe us, and he'll know it."

"He didn't come here naked, did he?"

The smile returned to Bull's face. "No, I don't suppose he did." He grabbed Dandy's face and stole a fast, deep kiss. "Well, what are waiting for? Let's go, boyo!"

They made their way back down to the first floor, careful to keep out of sight. They spied Mrs. Breem in the parlor with Jacques, and avoided it, cautiously creeping down a narrow hall to the coat closet. Bull slowly and quietly pulled the door open, and Dandy slipped inside.

He felt coat sleeves, letting his power show him their owners until he found the one belonging to the mayor. Reaching into the mayor's pocket, he retrieved a billfold and a pocket watch, and passed them to Bull.

Bull searched the billfold and found a card inside. He took it and the pocket watch, and gave the billfold back to Dandy, who replaced it in Forge's coat.

The two men returned to their room with their stolen prizes as cautiously as they'd come. They didn't breathe easily until they were back inside their suite and examining the card and pocket watch in the lantern light.

The card was imprinted with a name and address—Gideon Forge, Mayor, 100 N. Holliday St., Baltimore, Maryland.

Bull opened the pocket watch and read what was inscribed on the inside of the lid. "To my dear Gideon, forever yours, Clara." He looked up at Dandy. "Think it's his wife? I bet Clara won't be too glad to hear how her dear Gideon spends his Friday nights, eh?"

Dandy nodded. He suddenly looked down at himself, and laughed out loud.

"What's so funny, boyo?"

"It just occurred to me that this is the first time we picked a pocket stark naked!"

Bull looked stunned for a moment, then laughed as well. "So we are, me fine bucko. And even naked, we're the best in town." He snapped the pocket watch closed, and slipped it and the card into his jacket pocket. "And tomorrow, after we have a little chat with Gideon Forge, we'll be the richest pickpockets as well!"

Chapter Six

City Hall was an extravagant affair, perhaps the most ornate building Bull and Dandy had ever seen. Not even the new Tribune building in New York could match it. The Tribune was taller, of course, the clock tower soaring over two hundred and fifty feet into the air, but it wasn't as fancy as the domed, white marbled structure standing before them.

It was four stories high, the same as Club Raven, but the cupola rose much higher, and gleamed white under the sun. Its sheer grandeur made Dandy wonder if they were making a mistake. Surely any man who served as mayor in a building such as this could not be intimidated by a pair of Five Points pickpockets.

As if Bull read his mind, an elbow in the ribs startled him out of his thoughts. "He didn't build the damn thing, Dandy. He just works here."

"It's so...so...elegant, though."

"It's a building like any other, just a wee bit bigger and shinier is all."

"I suppose." Dandy nodded, almost to himself. "Okay, let's get on with it then." He led the way under the arches to the front doors, where he paused. They were fashioned from dark wood and intricately carved with leaves and flowers. "Do you suppose we knock or just go inside?"

"Them's knockers on the door, ain't they?" Bull pointed to a pair of huge brass doorknockers gleaming brightly against the dark wood. "Wouldn't be there if they wanted everyone to just walk inside."

Dandy picked one up and rapped it sharply against the door a couple of times. It was surprisingly heavy, and he could hear the sound echo inside.

The door cracked open, answered by a smartly dressed Negro. He pulled the door open wide and ushered them inside, closing it behind them. "May I direct you gent'men?"

"Um, we're here to see Gideon Forge," Dandy said. "He's the mayor."

Bull elbowed him again. "He knows who the mayor is, boyo."

"So? He asked and I'm telling." Dandy scowled. If Bull didn't stop shoving that sharp elbow into his ribs, he was going to bruise like an overripe apple.

The servant seemed to take no notice of their squabble. "Sirs, Mayor Forge's office is down this way. Please follow me, and I'll show you in." His shoe heels made smart clicking sounds on the marble floor as he headed off.

They followed behind him, trying not to gawk. It was difficult, though, especially as they passed through the center of the hall. The place was even more elaborate on the inside than it'd been on the outside. Dandy paused and craned his neck, looking up at the beautiful, gracefully domed skylight far above his head. Stately stone columns stretched upward from the ground floor, supporting the dome, and the glass skylight sparkled like a blue eye looking down at him. He realized he was being left behind and hurried to catch up.

The servant led them down a hallway to another pair of double doors. He knocked softly with a white-gloved hand, and waited until a voice within told him to enter. Opening the door, he ushered Bull and Dandy inside. "Visitors, sir. They say they have business with you." He gave Bull and Dandy a respectful nod and left, pulling the doors closed behind him.

The office was spacious, and richly appointed with polished, dark wood furniture and velvet upholstery, gleaming brass accents and sconces. The windows were festooned with heavy gold drapery, and a thick Persian rug graced the marble floor.

The mayor stood at the tall window directly behind his desk, staring out, his back to the door. He turned around as Bull and Dandy reached his desk. "Gentlemen, good day. What brings two such fine young men to City Hall today? I must tell you in advance that if you're collecting for your church or a charity, all donations must be submitted in writing to the City Council for consideration."

"We're not here for money," Bull said.

"Sure we are." Dandy nudged Bull. "That's exactly why we're here."

Bull tossed Dandy an exasperated look. "Will you let me do the talking, boyo?" He turned back to the mayor. "We've met before, us three."

"We have?" Forge looked from one to the other, his thick eyebrows knitting. "I fear I can't place you. Where have we met?"

"At the Soiled Dove only last night."

For the briefest of moments a look of pure shock coated Forge's features, but he covered it quickly, composing his expression into one of indignation. "I'm afraid I haven't the slightest understanding of what you are speaking about, young man. You must have me confused with someone else. I've heard of that dreadful place, and I've never—"

"Never what?" Bull's mouth slanted into a wicked grin. "Never went there? Never took off every last stitch of clothing? Never stood by with your pecker in your hand and watched me and my friend here fuck a pretty French geycat?"

Forge's face turned an angry shade of red, his cheeks mottling with color. "You will leave this office immediately, the pair of you, or I'll call for the constable!"

"Go ahead. Call one. Call ten. The more witnesses the better, I think." Dandy grinned at Forge and dug into his pocket, pulling out the card imprinted with Forge's name. "We got this last night at the Soiled Dove." He tossed it onto Forge's desk.

"Bah. You could've gotten my card at any one of a number of locations. I pass them out whenever I visit local businesses. It means nothing!"

"Maybe, but I'd bet my soul you don't go around leaving things· like this at every haberdashery or bank office you visit." Bull raised his hand and dangled the pocket watch from its fob chain. "And before you say it's not yours, I'd remind you of the inscription, bucko. 'To my dear Gideon, forever yours, Clara.' Sound familiar?"

"You...you stole it!"

"Of course we did. We took it while you were getting your cock sucked."

"I never!"

"You did, and there ain't no sense lying to us about it. Matter of fact, you made an offer to fuck us. Said you'd pay top dollar. Ain't that right, Dandy?"

"It is, indeed, Bull. I heard him. I also heard him call us low class. Now, I expect we should get an apology for that, yeah?"

"An apology? Nah, we don't need one of those. What we need are bills, lots of 'em. Say, five thousand of them?" Bull swung the pocket watch side to side like a pendulum. "Unless you want we should start telling people what you've been getting up to at the bawdy house."

Dandy nodded. "Yeah. I think Clara would be interested to hear the story, don't you, Bull?"

"Definitely."

Forge stammered and sputtered. "Y-you can't! You're bluffing. You wouldn't dare!"

"Oh, wouldn't we? We're rough and uneducated, ain't we? You said so yourself. We wouldn't know no better." Bull snorted, and tucked the watch back inside his pocket.

Forge growled, and leaned forward, bracing his meaty hands on the desktop. "Listen to me very carefully. You will leave that pocket watch here on my desk, and if you ever open your mouths to anyone, I'll have you arrested and thrown into prison."

Bull wagged a finger at Forge. "Not before we tell everyone you're nothing but a fat fairy. And they'll believe us. People always want to believe rumors, don't they? Especially about people they don't like. Word is, you're not a very popular mayor these days, bucko. Folks might want to kick your fat ass out of this office, and a rumor sayin' you like to fuck men would sure be a convenient reason to put you out like the family cat."

Forge's face faded from red to a sickly greenish color. "Five thousand is far too much. I don't have it."

"Yes, you do. If you lie to us again, the price goes up to ten thousand."

For a minute, Dandy was sure Forge was going to vomit all over his gleaming desk. "You'll have to give me time to get the money, then. I don't keep that much in my office safe."

Bull and Dandy exchanged a glance, then Dandy nodded. They'd discussed this part of the plan before they came here. "Sure, we'll give you time. You've got until noon tomorrow. We'll meet you at the Soiled Dove. Come alone, or we'll slip out the back door, and before suppertime everyone in Baltimore will know who you like to suck your dick."

"Including Clara," Bull put in.

"*Especially* Clara," Dandy added. "Which would be a shame, since it was her family's money that put you in this office, eh, bucko?" They'd found that out by talking to a couple of the prostitutes at the Soiled Dove late last night, after the party ended.

Forge sank onto his chair, which squealed under his weight, his hands gripping the edge of his desk so hard the knuckles whitened. "Are you through with me now? Please leave. I have things to do before I can go see my banker."

They both nodded at Forge, offering him a sarcastic tip of their hats before turning smartly and marching out of the office. Their pace was measured—they didn't want to hurry, giving him the impression they were afraid of being stopped, nor did they dawdle, not wanting to give him time to change his mind and start calling for a constable.

It wasn't until they were safely outside City Hall and mixing in with the crowd on the street that they would admit they'd gotten away with it, that their plan was working. By tomorrow afternoon, they'd be rich men!

"Come on, boyo. I'll buy you a hot lunch at that restaurant up the street from the Soiled Dove. I've worked up an appetite, I have."

Dandy's grin felt like it might split his face in half. "I can't believe it worked!"

"Of course it worked. We're a pair, ain't we? Think about it, Dandy. No more small potatoes. We're in the big time now!"

"How much money do you have? I want a great big steak, red and juicy, with potatoes."

Bull smirked at him. "Today we'll have whatever's less than a dollar. Come tomorrow afternoon, I'll buy you the whole damn cow."

Forge slammed his fist on top of his desk, funneling his fury into the motion. The elegant but sturdy desk, for all its superior craftsmanship and solidity, shuddered under the assault. "Where the fuck were you? I've been waiting here for hours!"

Detective Thomas Arthur Clare stood stoically in the face of Forge's tantrum, unmoved by the ferocity of Forge's mood. He tugged at a cuff and flicked a minute piece of lint from his plaid woolen suit. He prided himself on his appearance as much as he did his abilities as a detective. "I was at the scene of a murder. Quite an interesting case, actually. It seems a chambermaid was found dead in her employer's water closet—"

"I don't give a fig about some dead servant girl! When I send a courier to fetch you, I expect you to come immediately, not at your leisure."

Still unflappable, Clare tugged at his other cuff, straightening it. "What is it you require, Mayor Forge?"

Forge spoke through gritted teeth. "I require you to find two men. One is a stocky redhead, the other is taller and darker. Both are Irish. They called themselves 'Bull' and 'Dandy,' and they were last seen at a bawdy house called the Soiled Dove."

"What do you want with these two men?"

"That's my affair, and none of yours. I want you to find them, and kill them."

The order perked Clare's ears as nothing else said had since he'd entered the office. The sheer audacity of the mayor shocked him. "Mayor Forge, I must remind you I am a sworn officer of the law. I cannot and will not act as some sort of hired thug sent to murder men who have not been tried in court! The very idea is abhorrent."

Forge scowled so fiercely, deep lines wreathed his eyes, almost swallowing them completely. "Very well, very well. Arrest them then, and lock them up."

"On what charges?"

"They're liars and thieves, and I suspect them of being homosexuals. Those three charges are enough to see them sent away for the rest of their lives, although I'd be happier to see them swing from the end of a nice, sturdy rope."

Clare narrowed his eyes at Forge in suspicion. Instead of answers, Forge's response only raised more questions in Clare's keenly inquisitive mind. "Why these two? There are plenty of degenerates who make their homes here. What makes these two so special you wish to send me out personally to bring them in?"

"These two are low born, but they're smart. That's why I need you to go after them. They'll outwit the local constables far too easily, I'm afraid." He heaved himself out of his chair and stalked to the window, staring out, his beefy hands clasped behind his back. "As for why I want them...I have my reasons. Leave it at that."

Clare sighed, and took a small notebook out of his coat pocket, along with a pencil. He opened it and began to write. "You said their names are Bull and Dandy? And their last names, sir?"

"I haven't the slightest idea."

"I see. I think it safe to assume those aren't their true Christian names. Aliases, most likely. You said they might be found at the brothel called the Soiled Dove? That's Mrs. Breem's place, isn't it?"

"I don't know any woman by that name, and I believe that may be the name I heard for the establishment they frequent. I certainly don't make a habit of learning the names of every bawdy house in the city, Detective."

Forge remained facing the window, but Clare noticed the back of his neck mottled an ugly red at the mention of Mrs. Breem. *He's lying. He's familiar with the name, either of the place, the woman, or both.* "I believe you describe one as redheaded, and the other as taller and darker, correct? And you say these men are thieves? What is it they've stolen? Has a report been made by the victim of the alleged theft?"

"For God's sake, just go find them!" Forge roared, his voice echoing in the room. "I'm a very busy man and have no more time to discuss this matter with you. Go and do your job, or so help me, God, I'll have you fired immediately! You won't be able to get a job anywhere in this city, not even as a fucking rat catcher. Do I make myself clear, Detective?"

"Certainly, sir. I'll let you know when I've found them." Clare gave Forge a respectful nod before walking to the office door. He removed his hat from the table where he'd placed it upon entering, and set it firmly on his head before opening the door and taking his leave.

Mayor Forge is a most disagreeable man, Clare thought as he walked down the hallway toward the rotunda. *He is also not telling me the truth about these men, and that begs the question, "Why?" What have these two men done that makes him want them dead or thrown into prison for the rest of their lives? He was also sure to tell me they were liars, which isn't a punishable offense unless some sort of fraud is involved. It's obvious he doesn't want me to believe anything they might say to me. What they might say that has him so worried?*

Clare was intrigued by the mystery of the relationship between Mayor Forge and the two men he tasked Clare with finding, particularly since it involved Mrs. Breem's infamous Soiled Dove bawdy house.

He couldn't be more pleased. The assignment gave him the perfect excuse to see the inside of the Soiled Dove, something he'd been yearning to do since he first heard about its existence, but had been too fearful of his career to attempt. His cock woke, swelling at the very thought of what might go on inside the walls of Mrs. Breem's place. Rumor held it was a place of debauchery, where men had relations with men, and every taste, no matter how wicked, was accommodated.

By the time he hailed a carriage to take him to Lancaster Street where the Soiled Dove was located, a full erection was making him decidedly uncomfortable.

Chapter Seven

O h, dear! I'm quite certain you're mistaken, Detective Clare." Maude Breem, a delicate, older woman who was probably quite lovely in her day, fanned herself with a beautifully beaded silk fan. She seemed kind and hospitable, offering Clare tea and cake when he came to call on her. "My home is all I have since my beloved husband died. I take in gentlemen boarders by necessity, you see, to help meet my obligations. What you're suggesting...oh dear! I may faint." The fan flurried faster, and her hand shook as she raised a delicate china cup to her lips.

"My apologies, Mrs. Breem. I'm sorry to upset you so, but I'm sure you understand why I must ask these questions." Clare chose a square of lemon cake from the tray proffered by the butler. "The sooner I can clear up this misunderstanding, the sooner I can leave you to continue overseeing your business."

She sighed, a fragile sound, giving Clare the impression she was like a piece of paper-thin crystal capable of shattering at the slightest touch. "Of course, Detective Clare. You couldn't possibly know the truth if all you're told are lies. Tell me, who told you those awful stories? Was it those men at St. Luke's? They've hated me since I bought this building when my husband passed. They frown on women working outside the home, you see." Her smile was charming, and it lit her eyes. "Although I suppose I'm working *inside* the home, since I live here!"

He wasn't fooled by her for an instant. She was a good actress, but he'd interacted with better in the course of his years as a detective. She was trying to placate him, and play on his masculine sympathies by relating her story of being a poor widow trying to run a legitimate boarding house, clinging to her business despite the damage caused by evil, venomous rumors such as those he's heard. "I'm terribly sorry but I can't reveal the names of my sources. You understand anonymity is vitally important in these matters."

"Oh, yes, Detective. I certainly do understand."

Was she saying more than it appeared? If rumors were true, anonymity would certainly be important to her as well. He lifted his cup to his lips and drained the last of the tea as he considered her reply, then settled it carefully back on its saucer with a musical clink. "Well, thank you very much for the tea and cake. You've been most helpful. If you don't mind, I'll just have a quick inspection of the building, and we can clear this unfortunate matter off the books."

"Aninspection? You mean you want to go into the rooms? My dear sir, I can't have strangers wandering about, peeking into the rooms! It would be terribly inappropriate."

"I assure you, I will be most discreet. It's necessary, madam. Surely you wish to settle this matter once and for all? Although, if you feel so strongly about me touring the house by myself, I would be happy to return with uniformed constables..."

She fanned herself again. "No, no. That won't be necessary. I was thinking of my clients' privacy, you understand." She motioned to the butler. "Jacques, please escort Detective Clare through the house and open whatever rooms he wishes to enter. Be certain to knock first, in case my boarders are...indisposed."

Jacques nodded and opened the door, obviously waiting for Clare to exit.

Clare stood, and gave Maude a courtly bow. "My thanks again, Mrs. Breem. You've been most gracious."

She nodded at him, still fanning herself. He could feel her

gaze on him, burning, even through the fabric of his coat as he turned and walked out of the room. He could only imagine her fury at having to acquiesce to his demands. Despite her demur behavior, she didn't strike him as a woman who took disruptions to her business lightly.

If the Soiled Dove operated as rumor said it did, he hoped she wouldn't hold his insistence on inspecting the property against him since he'd want to plan an *unofficial* visit very soon.

Jacques led him first through the rooms on the ground floor. In addition to the parlor where Mrs. Breem had received Clare, there was a sewing room, a water closet, and the servants' quarters. A door there led out to the yard and another stone building in which the kitchen and smokehouse were located. A quick check on the servants' rooms proved them to be empty; the kitchen bustled with activity as the cook and maids worked to complete luncheon service which would be served at noon.

The second floor held a row of guest rooms along the left side of a long hallway. An immense ballroom took up the entire right side. The ballroom was empty, tables bare of linen, the floor gleaming and spotless. White sheets covered chairs and other odd pieces of furniture which seemed to have been stored in there, as if the ballroom was rarely, if ever, used.

They began walking up the hallway. Jacques knocked at each door—there were a half dozen according to Clare's count—and they waited a few moments either for the tenant to openit, or for Jacques to do. He noticed Jacques's knock was identical each time—three slow bangs against the wood. Clare looked away so Jacques wouldn't see the smirk on his face. It was obviously a signal to those within the room.

Male tenants opened three of the doors. To a one they expressed surprise and indignation at Clare's presence and insistence on inspecting their rooms, but reluctantly allowed him access. He gave a cursory search, but could find no evidence of wrongdoing in any of them, and left each one quickly.

Except for the finalroom.

No one answered Jacques' knock on the last door so, after a long few moments, Clare motioned for Jacque to unlock it. It was immediately apparent that someone was living here—*two* someones, in fact. Several articles of clothing were strewn on the bed and over a chair, and a quick look revealed they were of two distinctly different sizes. Whoever these men were, they seemed slovenly, and most of their clothes were worn or ill-made. They didn't strike Clare as the sort of men who Mrs. Breem would welcome into her boarding house.

The washing water on the dresser was dirty, and the towels damp. Someone had washed up rather recently, but there didn't seem to be anyone here for now. A peek under the bed revealed nothing but a couple of small dust clots, and a single shoe.

A single shoe. Where was its mate? Could it be that whoever was in the room was so startled by Jacques's knock that they left with one bare foot? If so, where did they go? He doubted they would've jumped from the second floor, and besides, when he checked the windows, all were locked.

As he pondered, his hand brushed against a jacket thrown casually across the dresser. A bulge in the pocket caught his attention, which proved to be a gold pocket watch. The inscription inside read, "To my dear Gideon, forever yours, Clara." Grinning, he snapped it shut and turned his full attention back to the room. They were here, the two men Forge had sent him after, and now he had proof of their thievery. But where were they hiding?

His gaze fell on a huge armoire set against the far wall of the bedroom. It was over six feet tall, ornate and beautifully crafted, and there were brightly polished brass pull knobs on its double doors. He smiled to himself as he walked over to it and pulled both doors open at once.

A pair of men, one dressed in pants but wearing only one shoe, the other in nothing but his underdrawers, tumbled out. The partially dressed man was slender, with dark hair and eyes, and the other was a stocky, well-built redhead.

Clare slipped a hand into his coat pocket and withdrew his Remington single action revolver, pointing it at the pair. "Would you boys happen to be Irish?"

Neither of them moved a muscle, both staring wide-eyed at the muzzle of Clare's gun.

"Come now, boys. I'm not going to shoot you for answering my questions. Are you Irish?"

"Y-yeah, we are, both of us. What's it to you, bucko?" The redhead's tone was belligerent even though he sat like stone, his gaze still pinned to the gun in Clare's hand.

"What are your names?"

"I'm Bull, and this here is me friend, Dandy."

Clare smiled. "I have the feeling you're the two men for whom I've been searching." He turned to Jacques. "Please inform Mrs. Breem that I'll be arresting these two men and escorting them to the city jail. I apologize for any inconvenience this may cause her." He motioned toward Bull and Dandy with his gun. "All right, you two. Get up, slowly. Keep your hands up where I can see them."

"What for?" Bull demanded, baring his teeth at Clare. He was a firebrand, for sure, and almost made Clare smile. "Sure and we ain't done nothing."

"You're being charged with theft, more specifically, with picking the mayor of Baltimore's pocket. I believe you stole this." He held up the pocket watch, swinging it by its fob chain. He watched their faces carefully, and was rewarded when both of them averted their eyes, a sign of guilt in his mind. "Let's go."

He marched them out of the room at the point of his gun, and directly out of the building. He caught sight of Mrs. Breem standing in the parlor doorway, a handkerchief clutched in her hand held to her mouth, but ignored her. Perhaps he'd send her a nice spray of flowers or chocolates later to make amends for interrupting her business. For now, it was imperative to see his prisoners secured in jail cells.

Jacques hailed a cab for them, then quietly retreated into the house. As for the prisoners, they continued to protest their innocence during the cab ride to the jail, throughout the processing procedure where they were stripped and given threadbare, black and white striped prison uniforms and brogan boots, and continued to do so even as the cell door slammed shut behind them.

"Save your breath, boys. If the mayor has his way, you'll be in here until you're both old and gray." Clare almost felt badly for them. The jail was filthy, damp, and about as abysmal a place as a man could imagine. The cells were fashioned of bare stone, and barely six feet wide. Prisoners were worked hard, and fed little. The mayor might have them sentenced to life, but if God was merciful it would be a short one.

Personally, he didn't feel theft of a damned pocket watch was a serious enough offense to warrant a life sentence, and during his talk with Forge, he'd become convinced there was something else going on. He leveled a steady glare at the dark-haired man, the one called Dandy. Between the two, he seemed the more likely to cooperate. "If you answer some questions, I might be able to convince the mayor a lighter sentence is in order."

"Don't do it, Dandy." Bull shoved a shoulder into Dandy's arm. "The law ain't never helped us, boyo."

"Listen to me, Dandy. All I want to know is if the mayor is telling me the entire truth about what happened. Where were you when you stole the pocket watch?"

Dandy blinked, and chewed on his lower lip. "We was at—"

"Dandy!" Bull shoved Dandy, rocking him on his feet.

"What are you doing, boyo? You know what they'd do to us if they found out what we was up to that night?" He circled his hand around his throat.

Dandy's eyes grew wide and round. "Fuck! I almost..."

Bull growled at him. "Just keep your fucking mouth shut, yeah?"

Clare scowled at the two of them. "Listen, I *know* there's something else going on, something that has to do with you, the Mayor, and Maude Breem. I suggest you tell me the truth now, or things will go even worse for you later on."

"We ain't got nothing more to say." Bull took Dandy's elbow and dragged him toward the back of the cell where a pair of bare, wooden pallets waited. They sat side by side, and stared at the stone wall opposite them.

Clare grumbled under his breath. *Fine. Let them sit and stew. Maybe a few days breaking their backs swinging sledgehammers on the chain gang will convince them to talk to me.* He left without speaking again.

Chapter Eight

Days passed before Tony caught wind of what had happened to Bull and Dandy. They'd disappeared from Club Raven with a sack full of billfolds and silver, destroying every hope Tony had and undermining his belief that anyone could rise above their humble beginnings if given the opportunity.

He'd given them everything, and they'd failed him. It infuriated him, and he spent the time in a sour mood, sulking around his apartment, rarely speaking with anyone. Then he began to question his anger. After all, when he'd first come to Club Raven he hadn't believed his good fortune, either. He'd begun hiding away small treasures from around the Club—silver snuff boxes, coins carelessly left lying on tables by guests, a gold cufflink he found on one of the sofas in the Great Room. He made certain everything he took was small and easy to hide, easy to transport.

He prepared himself for what he believed was inevitable—that something would go wrong, that he'd be thrown out. The difference between him and Bull and Dandy was that, while he was ready for what he saw as an eventuality, he didn't act prematurely. He was determined to enjoy everything offered to him until the moment it was taken away. Bull and Dandy hadn't stayed long enough to benefit from anything Tony had to give them. He didn't understand, and the puzzle was driving him crazy.

When he finally got word of them, it came from the least

likely of sources—his mother.

He looked up as the door to his apartment opened and his mother backed inside, carrying a silver tray loaded with covered dishes. "Mama, I told you I'm not hungry."

"*Non discutere con tua madre. Sei troppo magro. Hai bisogno di mangiare.*" She scowled at him and walked across the room to place the tray on the small table set against a window. When she lifted the lid of one of the dishes, the delicious smell of cheesy pasta drifted over and his stomach growled despite his protestations.

"I'm not arguing, Mama, and I'm not skinny. I eat."

"*Non abbastanza.*"

He smiled for the first time since Dandy and Bull ran off. "More than enough. You're making me fat!"

She waved a hand at him and waited by his chair, fully expecting him to obey her.

As always, he did. When he sat, she tucked a white linen napkin into his shirt collar, draping it across his chest. The tray held a dish of lasagne, a small dish of grated cheese, and a bowl of minestrone soup. He picked up a spoon and sampled the soup. "Delicious, Mama. As always."

She nodded, then sat on the edge of the bed. It was obvious she wasn't leaving until she made sure he ate. God love her, his mother could be frustratingly maternal sometimes.

Silence at mealtimes was not something most Italian families observed, at least not in Tony's experience, and this was no exception. His mother began chatting, telling him about her day. He listened with half an ear until one particular sentence made his hand freeze with the soup spoon halfway to his mouth. "What did you say?"

Maria cocked her head toward him. "*Ho detto, il mio amico, Lucia, lavora come cuoco per la prigione. Mi ha detto che quei due ragazzi che hai avuto qui, gliquelli irlandesi, sono in là.*"

He rested the spoon on the bowl, and turned to look at her. "Your friend, Lucia, who cooks for the prisoners at the jail, said she saw Bull and Dandy there? The Irish boys who were staying here?"

She nodded, and motioned with an impatient flip of her hand for him to continue eating. "*Sì. Dove altro sarebbero? Hanno rubato l'argento.*"

"I know they stole the silver, Mama, but I don't think they need to be in jail. You remember how it was back in Five Points. You know how hard it is to trust anyone."

Her sigh and nod told him she did. Then she shrugged. "*Beh, almeno finire di mangiare prima.*"

He tilted his head and blinked at her. "Finish eating before I do what?"

"*Prima di andare loro ottenere.*"

Tony laughed. Sometimes his mother knew him better than he knew himself. "You're right again, Mama. I'll eat, then go get them."

She smiled at him, stood up, and pinched his cheek, then left the room, no doubt content that he'd do exactly as he promised.

He stared down at the food, wondering if she'd notice if he didn't eat, then figured it would be better to hurry and swallow it all than suffer the tongue lashing she'd give him later on. Besides, he was actually feeling better than he had in days, and his appetite seemed to be coming back.

As he tucked in, his mind tried to pick apart the puzzle of what had happened. He, above all people, understood why Bull and Dandy might've felt the need to steal, but where had they gone after, and why had they ended up in jail? It wasn't over the billfolds and silver taken from Club Raven—Tony had used his powers to cover the thefts up, and certainly hadn't reported them to the police.

Had Bull and Dandy robbed someone else after leaving Club

Raven? Why, when if they pawned what they'd taken, they'd have enough money to sustain them comfortably for at least a month?

By the time he'd cleaned his plate, he was no closer to answers than when he'd begun, but he was determined to get them. He quickly washed up, then put on his coat, grabbed his walking stick, and headed downstairs.

The driver pulled his horses to halt outside the building where the city jail was located. Tony paid the driver and asked him to wait before alighting from the carriage. The building was imposing, a stone structure that seemed cold and brutal, even from the outside. He squared his shoulders and went inside.

It took him a while to secure a meeting with someone named Captain More, who claimed to be in charge of prisoners at the jail, and even longer to convince Captain More to release Bull and Dandy into Tony's care.

"Now, see here, Mister Brazzio, I can't be responsible for releasing those two prisoners into lawful society. The mayor himself ordered them put away. Says they're dangerous, maniacs, he called them. Who would question the word of a great man like Mayor Forge? Not you or me, I'd wager."

In the end, it took a hefty bribe and a dose of Tony's talent to get Captain More to change his mind, although Tony cared less about the money than he did about the time spent arguing his case. He was anxious to get Bull and Dandy back under Club Raven's protective roof. If the mayor was truly behind their incarceration, then the trouble they'd gotten into was worse—and far more dangerous—than he'd thought. Mayor Forge was an influential man in Baltimore, who had the power of the law behind him.

He waited, his impatience growing with each passing moment like a sponge set in a basin of water. Standing, he began to pace back and forth, drawing disapproving frowns from constables and curious stares from other people who sat on the long, hard bench provided in the waiting area.

Not that he gave one whit what anyone thought of him, but the longer he waited, the more he worried that Forge had been told Tony came to get Bull and Dandy, and the more positive he became that he'd be the next one in chains.

He'd never allow that to happen, of course. He'd have to use his power more liberally than ever, and in doing so might jeopardize the secrecy so important to Club Raven's success. Julian and Matthias would be incredibly upset, and the last thing he wanted was to get on their bad side. He might have to leave Club Raven, give up his inheritance, and then where would he be? Where would his mother live. How would they survive?

Just as he thought his last nerve was going to snap and his brain explode in a fit of apoplexy, he spied two familiar figures in the doorway. Although they wore regular clothing—albeit wrinkled and torn in a few places—their hands were handcuffed behind their backs. Both of them sported bruises on their faces, and from the smug expression on the face of the guard who accompanied them, Tony had no doubt who put them there.

"Why are these men shackled?" He swore under his breath in Italian as he stalked over to them. "Release them at once!"

The officer's lip curled over his teeth, his nose wrinkling as if he smelled something foul in the air. "The captain said some Italian was waiting to take possession of these two. You him?" He turned his head and spat on the ground. "Don't know why the captain trusts you. Italians and Gypsies, they're all the same. Can't trust the lot of you. Throw curses and whatnot at law abiding folk, that's what me sainted mother used to say."

Tony swallowed his fury at the ignorant double ethnic slur,

and held out his hand. "Give me the key." He pushed a bit of his power into the officer's head, resisting the urge to push *all* of it in and hope the force would be enough to make the officer's skull explode.

The officer looked confused, but quickly lay a metal skeleton key on Tony's palm. "I...I need that and the cuffs back. Don't be thinking of stealing them."

"Aw, he's rich, Brady! He don't need your stinkin' key and bracelets." Bull jangled the cuffs on his wrists. "He could buy and sell you a dozen times, bucko, and that's the truth."

"Could he now?" Anger flashed in Brady's eyes.

Tony noticed another officer walking closer, fingering the billy club tucked into his belt. He pushed Brady a little harder, and was rewarded by the clink of the handcuff locks opening.

The boys rubbed their wrists and looked at Tony. Dandy spoke first. "You sprung us, huh?"

"I did."

"Well, thanks. I mean, after what we done and all..." Dandy flinched when Bull elbowed him.

"Boyo, your mouth is winning the race against your brain again!"

Dandy growled at Bull, and gave him a push. "He'd be stupid not to know it was us what took the—"

"All right, boys, all right!" Tony cut in before Dandy could admit to the theft at Club Raven in full hearing of a half dozen police officers. "Let's get back, and get a hot meal into you. We can talk about it afterward. I'd wager you're half-starved, and I *know* you can both use a good scrubbing."

He grabbed their elbows and practically pulled them out of the station before they could give the police cause to throw them back into a cell.

True to the driver's word, the carriage was still waiting out front, and he directed Bull and Dandy to it. They clambered up, both choosing to sit on one side. He took the opposite cushion, the one facing forward, and motioned to the driver. "Club Raven again, and hurry. Night will be falling soon. It's growing cold already and none of us are dressed for it. We'll catch a chill."

That was the sum of conversation on the carriage ride back to the club. All three sat in silence, staring at the buildings and people as they passed. He didn't know what Bull and Dandy were thinking, but for himself, he was wondering what he was going to tell Julian and Matthias, or indeed if he needed to tell them anything at all. There'd been no harm done so far, except for a few pilfered odds and ends. Certainly nothing to cause Club Raven any hardship.

He supposed his silence would depend on the choices Bull and Dandy made from this point forward, and of course, what damage—if any—they'd done while out in the city. He still didn't know why Mayor Forge was so anxious to keep them in jail, and he only hoped it was nothing that would lead back to Club Raven.

If it was, then Bull and Dandy's future at the club—as well as his own—might be forfeit.

By the time they arrived back at Club Raven, the three of them were shivering. The night was brisk and, without top coats, the wind had chilled through and through. They hurried inside, and Tony led them straight through the building and out the back, into the kitchen in the courtyard.

Once inside, the three of them went directly to the large fireplace and huddled in front of it, letting the heat from the crackling flames chase the chill from their bones.

Mama Brazzio looked up from the stove where she stood stirring a large pot. "*Antonio? Sono questi gli uomini che hai portato da* Five Points?"

Tony nodded without turning from the warmth of the fire. "Yes, Mama. These are the ones I brought from Five Points. This is Bull, and this is Dandy. Boys, this is my mother, Maria Brazzio."

"*Che tipo di nome è 'Bull'*?"

Tony shrugged. "I don't know...it means a bull, Mama. You know, *un toro.*"

She held a finger up from each side of her head. "*Un toro*?" Laughing, she shook her head and clucked her tongue. "*E l'altro, Dandy? Cosa significa?*"

Tony thought for a moment. "Dandy means somebody who likes to dress up, and strut around proud of himself, I guess."

"Ah. *Come un pavone?*"

Tony laughed. "Yes, Mama. Like a peacock."

"Hey! I'm not a peacock!" Dandy huffed, his face mottling red.

"Yeah," Bull put in. "Quit telling your old lady tales about us. It ain't right, not while we're both standing right here. We don't know what she's saying—we can't talk that Eye-talian stuff."

Tony sighed. "I apologize. I was trying to explain your names to my mother. She's not used to nicknames like Bull and Dandy. She's used to calling people by an abreviated version of their names—like Tony is short for Anthony."

"Well, it ain't right to make fun."

Tony nodded. "I agree, and I'm sorry. Let's sit down. I'm sure my mother has something delicious in that pot over there."

Dandy seemed to forget all about his perturbance over Tony poking fun at his name. "Good, I'm starving. They didn't feed us enough in jail to keep a sparrow alive."

"Yeah, and what they *did* give us tasted like horse manure," Bull added. "I think they shovel it off the streets straight onto our plates."

"Well, I guarantee whatever my mother serves you will not

taste like that!" Tony paused and translated for his mother, who cried out and shook her head. "Her food is always delicious."

She smiled as she placed steaming bowlfuls of soup in front of each of them, then added another basket piled high with thick slices of fresh bread. *"Mangiare! Siete tutti troppo magro.."*

"She says to eat, we're all too skinny."Tony grinned. "She thinks everyone is too skinny. I could weigh as much as an ox, and she'd still think I needed to eat more."

"That's okay with me, Missus!" Bull laughed and grabbed a piece of bread, tearing it into hunks. He dipped one in the soup and shoved it into his mouth. "This is good!"

A hand boxed his ear. He grabbed it and looked up to see Maria glaring at him. *"Non parlare con la bocca piena. Non è educato."*

Tony supressed a grin. "Mama says not to talk with your mouth full. It's not polite."

Bull rubbed his ear. "Sweet Jaysus, she don't have to beat me to—"

Maria boxed his other ear. "Ow!

"Prendere il nome del Signore invano!" Maria waggled her finger at Bull, and then at Dandy, who was sniggering over his soup.

"What was that one for?" Bull asked. His eyebrows were knit in an angry red knot.

"You took the Lord's name in vain." Tony put down his spoon, and looked at his mother. "Mama, leave us for a few minutes, please? I'll talk to them."

She huffed, but nodded and left the kitchen. After she was gone, Bull and Dandy turned to Tony with unasked questions in their eyes. He held up a hand before they could speak.

"Mama remembers how hard life was back in Five Points. She knows, as I do, that if you're going to live here at Club Raven then you need to become different men from the ones you were back in New York. You need to become educated and cultured to be accepted."

"Yeah? Well, who says we *want* to live here? We left once, we'll do it again." Bull growled, his gaze cold and hard.

"Yes, you left once, stole some billfolds and ran off with the silver, and where did that get you?" Tony arched an eyebrow. "In jail."

Dandy glanced sideways at him. "That wasn't our fault, yeah? We was ratted out."

Tony tapped the table with his forefinger. "I don't know what happened or what you did, but I do know that if you've made an enemy of Gideon Forge, he won't stop looking for you. Step outside this club, and he'll have you collared and thrown back in that cell, and this time I won't be able to get you out."

Bull sat back, folding his arms across his chest. "Why do you want to help us, anyway? We stole your silver!"

"I don't care about the silver. Look, I've told you this story before, and it's all true. I was nothing once, a hoodlum from Five Points, just like you two. I was given an opportunity to rise above my beginnings, and I succeeded, but that's not enough for some people. I want to prove that anyone can become a gentleman if given the opportunity, that it doesn't take breeding. That's why I brought you from New York, and it's why I bailed you out of jail.

"Now, I want you to listen to what I have to say very carefully, because this offer will not be repeated again. If you choose to leave, I won't stop you, but you'll be on your own from this moment forward. Whatever happens to you will be your own doing, understand?"

They nodded at Tony, their expressions wary.

"Good. If you stay, I will teach you everything you need to know to move through the upper rung of society as if you were born to it. You'll be given fine clothes, elocution lessons, and you'll be given positions with Club Raven. If you choose to work elsewhere, I'll make sure you have a glowing recommendation and references. Now, what do you say?"

Dandy tipped his chin up. "What do you get from this?"

"I'll be proven right. It will validate my own struggles, and remind people one doesn't need to be born upper class to be a gentleman."

Dandy and Bull exchanged a long look. "Bull, Forge is gonna be looking for us. That detective fella, too. We don't have no money, and we can't go back to Maude Breem's. That's the first place they'll look for us."

"You were at the Soiled Dove?" Tony was surprised. He didn't think Maude would take in a pair of ruffians like Bull and Dandy. "Were you hired on there?"

Bull rolled his eyes. "Naw, we was paying guests. Had the money from the silver and billfolds. Mrs. Breem, she was a good 'un." He cocked his head. "How do you know her? You don't seem the sort to go slumming in brothels."

Tony smiled. "We know Maude Breem well. We've done business with her before. Mostly to bring in some of her employees for our special guests' benefit."

Bull's mouth popped open. "You know what sort of goings on happen at the Soiled Dove, then?"

"Of course. What do you suppose happens upstairs at Club Raven? We offer the same amenities; we simply serve a different class of people. Maude entertains workingclass men, and small business owners. Our guests are from some of the richest and most powerful families in Maryland. We are very discriminating with our membership."

Dandy blew out a breath as if he'd been holding it. "Sweet Jay...er...Jaybird." He glanced around to see if Maria was in earshot, but she hadn't returned to the kitchen yet. "I thought this place was just about folks who had powers like we do."

"It is, but its more than that, too." Tony picked up his spoon. "Now, our soup is getting cold. What's your decision?"

They exchanged a look again, then Bull nodded at Tony. "Okay. If you promise to keep your word, we'll stay. Oh, and we may be in a wee bit of trouble with the law. A detective named Clare was after us, sent by the mayor. Think you can call him off our tails?"

"I suppose. Maybe you better tell me what happened with the mayor to get him so angry in the first place." Tony relaxed at hearing they were willing to stay, and began to eat again.

As they ate, Bull and Dandy took turns telling Tony their story, including details of the party at the Soiled Dove, recognizing the mayor through Dandy's power, and trying to extort money from Forge.

Maria wandered back into the kitchen, and the three men exchanged a knowing glance. "We can continue this discussion later, upstairs. You can join me in my room for a nightcap," Tony said. They finished eating in relative silence, but Tony was already making plans for what he now knew had to be done.

The first thing Tony needed to do was find this Detective Clare, and figure out a way to make him lose interest in Bull and Dandy. After that, he needed to figure out what to do about the mayor. Additionally, he needed to come up with a plan to turn a pair of Irish street rats into polished gentlemen.

He decided he'd head over to Maude Breem's establishment that very evening to see if she had any information she could share on the subject of Thomas Clare.

One thing was for sure—from now on, his life was not going to be dull.

Chapter Nine

This fucking idiot let them walk right out of the prison!"
Gideon Forge wasn't known for minding his temper,
and at the moment it was roaring through his office un-
checked. He banged his meaty fists on his desk, making inkwells
and ashtrays bounce and rattle. His voice, as big as the rest of
him, echoed in the room, bouncing off walls like a solid, living
thing.

More terrifying than his temper was the power at his fingertips, and Officer Cal Brady feared what Gideon could do to him
as much as anyone did. Never in his life had he quailed before
another man, but in the face of Gideon Forge's anger, he shook
like a leaf in a storm. "Mayor Forge, please...I—"

"Shut up!" Gideon picked up an inkwell and flung it at Brady's
head. Brady ducked just in time. It sailed past and shattered on
the wall behind, splattering the wall with black ink. "You stupid
ignoramus! You had one job, to keep two lowlife miscreants in
a jail cell, but what happens? The minute some bleeding heart
asshole comes in and asks, you release them!"

"No, no, it wasn't like that. He talked to the captain. It's the
cap's fault!" He looked wildly from Forge to Captain More, who
stood off to the side and looked like he wished he were anywhere but here.

More shook his head. "Not me. I never said such a thing to
anybody. You been drinkin' again, Brady?"

Brady gasped. "I never touch a drop, so help me! I've been
as dry as the Sahara since last June. Ask me wife if you don't
believe me!"

"Shut up, the two of you!" Forge roared. His face was a ghastly shade of red, and his eyes bulged. "I ought to fire the both of you and be done with it, and I would if there was anybody better than a halfwit who wanted your jobs." He pointed at Brady. "You, get your fat ass back down to the cells and make sure no other prisoners walk out of your fucking jail."

Brady made a dash for the door, eager to get out before Forge changed his mind and fired him. The door hadn't quite closed behind him when he heard Forge order More to find Detective Clare and get him to Forge's office immediately.

Thomas stood quietly, staring out of a window in the mayor's office while Forge ranted and railed about someone named Brazzio bailing the Irishmen Thomas had arrested out of jail. When Forge finally ran out of breath, wheezing like a B&O steam engine, Thomas turned away from the window.

Thomas kept his voice low and level, but there would be no mistaking the menace in it. "Do I look like a fool to you, Mayor Forge?"

"What?"

He braced his hands on Forge's desktop, his gaze boring into Forge. "I asked if I look like a fool to you?"

Forge leaned away, his eyes widening. "Why, no! Of course not, Detective Clare. I was simply, er...venting my frustration at the incompetence of the uniformed constables at the jail. Why, Captain More's head has no more brains than a gourd. I wasn't inferring you were to blame in any way. More—"

"Then tell me why these two Irishmen are so important to you. And don't lie to me this time. It's not because they stole some bauble of yours."

Forge's thick lips flapped for a moment, as if they couldn't quite wrap themselves around the answer. Then he grimaced and avoided Thomas's gaze. "Fine. They *did* steal my pocket watch, the one my wife gave me on our tenth wedding anniversary. It's gold, mind you, worth quite a bit, and inscribed with both our names, but that's not what concerns me. It's *where* they stole it that's the more pressing problem."

Now they were getting closer to the truth. He could feel it coming, and nodded encouragingly. "Go on."

"I...First I must have your word that what I tell you will be held in the strictest of confidences."

"Of course, Mayor Forge. I work for you—you have my word of honor, sir."

Forge still looked hesitant to speak whatever was on his mind, but he took a deep breath and seemed to come to a decision. "Very well. They stole it from my jacket while I was... otherwise occupied...at the Soiled Dove."

Otherwise occupied? Ah, that explains so much! No wonder Forge was less than anxious to tell me where he was, and more than determined to get Bull and Dandy back here where he could silence them! "Maude Breem's place? The bawdy house?"

Forge nodded, and looked away, his cheeks pinking uponce again.

Thomas decided to rub a little salt in that particular wound. "You were there in an official capacity, I take it?"

"Of course not! How would it look to my constituents if their mayor was seen in a brothel?" His hands clenched into fists. It looked as if anger was flushing away his embarrassment. "We always take extreme precautions to protect our identities! If those two street rats hadn't come across my pocket watch, they would never have known I was there. They had one of my business cards, too, but of course, I destroyed that."

"You've already reassumed possession of the watch."

"Yes, I have it safely put away where it's unlikely to cause a problem like this again."

I notice he doesn't claim to be new to the Soiled Dove, nor that he plans never to return, Clare thought. His smile was wry, although he didn't enlighten Forge as to its cause. "Why do you care about these two men, then? Without the watch, it's their word against yours. Surely the good people of Baltimore would take the word of their mayor over a pair of Irish hoodlums?"

"I suppose they would, but I can't take the chance. Good God, Clare! Don't you understand what sort of house Maude Breem runs? This is an election year. If any of my opponents caught wind of my presence there..." His voice trailed off, but his meaning was crystal clear. He would never get reelected if anyone suspected he had sex with other men. "You understand now why I want them found dead or alive, and preferably the former?"

Thomas nodded. He understood completely. "I will find them and bring them in, but I will not kill them, Mayor Forge, not for love or money, not unless my own life or that of someone else may be forfeit if I don't shoot. Do *you* understand *that?*"

Forge looked relieved, although perhaps not as much as he might've been had Thomas agreed to murder the two Irishmen in cold blood. "Of course, of course. Now, the man who bailed them out of jail is namedAnthony Brazzio. I discreetly asked a few people about him. He's one of the owners of Club Raven. You've heard of the place?"

Thomas nodded. He had indeed. Club Raven was arguably the most exclusive men's club in Baltimore. Someone like him, or even the mayor, could never hope to afford a membership there. It was reserved for railroad tycoons and shipping magnates and the like. What an owner would want with a pair of thieves like Bull and Dandy was a mystery that intrigued him. Even simply seeing the inside of the place would be worth going to have a talk with Anthony Brazzio, although he didn't hold out hope of finding Bull and Dandy. If they had even half a brain between them, they'd be long gone from Baltimore by now. "I'll take a carriage over there. I'll report in tomorrow to let you know what I find out."

Forge seemed to regain some of his former bluster. He tapped his forefinger on his desk blotter. "Bring them back here to this office. I want to have a talk with them before I send them back to prison."

A talk that no doubt will end with a blade or a bullet, Thomas thought. There was no chance he'd be party to murder, and that's exactly what he would be if he allowed Forge to kill Bull and Dandy. He firmly believed that was exactly what Forge had in mind, thinking the office of mayor would offer protection from prosecution.

It would, too. Two men nobody cared about, who amounted to little, indeed who were strangers to Baltimore? No one would care if they turned up dead, floating in the Chesapeake Bay, nor would anyone try to find out who murdered them. They'd be buried in paupers' graves, and forgotten. Forge would easily get away with murder.

No, Thomas would figure out what to do with Bull and Dandy if he found them, but bringing them back to Forge was out of the question. In the meantime, he was going to take advantage of the opportunity to get a look see at Club Raven. "I'll be in touch."

"Yes. Don't forget to—"

He left without waiting for Forge to finish his sentence.

Once outside, he pulled his collar up against the chill and hailed a carriage. Climbing in, he gave the driver the address for Club Raven, and settled back for the ride.

Although it wasn't a very long trip, he was thoroughly chilled and very glad to see the imposing, four-story building that housed Club Raven come into view. The carriage stopped, and after he paid the driver he hopped out, wasting no time going to the doors at the entrance.

As cold as he was, he took a moment to compose himself, then lifted one of the heavy brass knockers and prepared to rap it smartly against the wooden door.

Just as he was about to knock, the door opened and a darkly handsome man rushed out, nearly bowling Thomas over. "Oh, pardon me! I didn't see you there." The man grabbed Thomas's elbow to steady him.

"No need to concern yourself. I'm fine." Thomas cocked his head, studying the man. Dark hair and eyes, olive complexion, fine clothes, gold-handled walking stick... "You wouldn't happen to be Anthony Brazzio, would you?"

Those intriguing dark eyes widened with surprise. "Why, I am, indeed. Who might you be, sir? I don't believe we've met."

"No we haven't." Thomas reached into his pocket and pulled out his badge. "I'm Detective Thomas Arthur Clare, Baltimore Police. I actually came here tonight to see you. I need to ask you a few questions."

Surprisingly, Anthony Brazzio smiled at him and stuck out a hand to shake. "I'm very pleased to meet you, Detective Clare. I've heard a great deal about you."

Thomas was taken aback, but recovered quickly. He took Brazzio's hand, shaking it. It was warm and strong and, to his great embarrassment, he found himself not wanting to let it go. "Erm, you have? May I ask from whom?"

"Of course. From two young men with whom I believe we're both acquainted. Please, it's cold out here. Let's go inside. There's a fire in the great room, and I'll have some brandy poured to warm our bones."

He was talking about Bull and Dandy! Were they still here? Thomas felt torn. He wanted to demand to know where Bull and Dandy were, but at the same time the offer to sit near a fire and drink brandy with Anthony Brazzio was tempting. Too tempting, as it turned out. He nodded and returned Brazzio's smile with one of his own. "That sounds fine, Mr. Brazzio. I accept your gracious offer."

"Please, call me Tony." He pushed the door open and ushered Thomas inside. "This way, please. Walther?"

A smiling black man in a neatly pressed tailcoat appeared almost as if by magic. "Yes sir, Mr. Tony?"

"Fetch us some brandy, will you? Is there anyone in the great room?"

"Yes, sir. Two or three of the members are in there, smokin' their cigars."

"Damn." Tony frowned, and turned toward Thomas. "I'm afraid we won't be free to speak if we sit in the great room. Too many ears to overhear our conversation."

Thomas nodded, hiding his disappointment.

Tony seemed to brighten. "If you don't mind, I'll have a fire lit in my apartment, and we can have our brandy there."

A chance to see one of the owner's private suites? Thomas would certainly not say no to that! He smiled and nodded. "That would be fine."

"Excellent." Tony turned to Walther. "Have a fire started, and bring the brandy up there."

Walther nodded, and reached for Tony's coat. He looked at Thomas. "May I take your coat, sir?

Thomas shrugged out of his great coat, glad he'd tucked his revolver in its holster under his suit jacket instead of keeping it in his pocket as he usually did. He let Walther take his coat, then followed Tony into the grand foyer.

"Have you ever visited us before?" Tony asked.

"No, I'm afraid I haven't had the opportunity, although I've heard much about it."

Tony smiled at him again. Every time, it seemed Tony's grin

grew brighter, until Thomas felt it could light a room without benefit of candle or gas lamp. "Then let me show you around before we retire to my suite. It'll give the fire time to warm the rooms."

Thomas tried not to appear overeager, but it was difficult to contain his excitement. "That would be most interesting. I don't mind saying I'm more than curious."

Tony showed him through a door to the right of the entry. It opened into a large room made cozy by a crackling fire in a huge stone fireplace. Framed portraits hung on the walls, along with a few taxidermied, mounted trophies, and plaques. Several men, all obviously affluent judging by their clothing, sat in over-stuffed chairs, smoking cigars and sipping at snifters. "This is the great room. As you can see, it's where our members gather to relax, play chess, smoke cigars, and enjoy a fine glass of sherry or brandy as the mood strikes them."

"It's a lovely room."

"It is." Tony nodded to a few of the gentlemen who took notice of them, then led Thomas out of the room. They walked across the foyer to a door on the opposite side. Tony held it open for Thomas to pass through.

It led to an immense dining hall. Tables dressed with fine white linen were crowned with colorful sprays of fragrant flowers. Tall red candles in silver holders added their light to that thrown by wall sconces. Golden ramekins and salt and pepper shakers gleamed in the candlelight. Thomas noticed even the plates were trimmed in gold.

"This is our members-only dining room. We offer a full selection of fine wines, and our chef is incomparable. I believe today's selection is pheasant. Are you hungry, Detective? I could have a plate sent up."

"No, no, thank you."

"Very well. This way, please." Tony led him through the dining room to an exit in the back. They walked through a service area where waiters were busily stacking dishes, and out the rear door, and into a secondary building in the courtyard. "This is our main kitchen. We serve up to one hundred people on a busy day."

A short, round woman with black hair woven into a braid circling her head looked up and smiled at them. "*Antonio! Sei venuto a mangiare?*"

Tony laughed. "No, mama, I'm not here to eat." He turned to Thomas. "Detective Clare, may I introduce my mother, Maria Brazzio. Mama, this is Detective Clare of the Baltimore Police."

She looked stricken, and pulled a pair of rosaries from her pocket, crossing herself with the crucifix. "*Polizia? Che cosa hai fatto, Antonio?*"

"I haven't done anything, Mama. Detective Clare is here to ask me a few questions, that's all. We'll be taking brandy up in my suite." He looked at Thomas again. "I'm sorry. We're originally from Five Points in New York, and the police weren't exactly friendly to the Italian immigrants up there."

Five Points? How did a kid who grew up in one of the worst slum areas of Manhattan come to be part owner in one of the most exclusive men's clubs in Baltimore? Thomas's curiosity burned hotter than ever.

Maria didn't speak again, but her gaze never left Thomas. He detected a sharp mind behind those dark eyes, and began to feel distinctly uncomfortable under her scrutiny. Tony must've noticed.

"Come, Detective, let's go. The suite must be warming up quite nicely by now, and I'll wager Walther is waiting for us with our brandies."

He nodded andfollowed Tony out of the kitchen, grateful to be out from under Maria's gaze.

"I apologize for my mother," Tony said as soon as they were

outside, out of earshot. "She's usually much more friendly than this."

"Don't apologize. I'm sure it must have been difficult living in Five Points. I've been there once. It was...chaotic."

Tony laughed. "That's a good word for it."

"Might I ask—"

Tony held his hand up, still grinning. "Oh, now, now, Detective. No questions until we're comfortably seated in my suite before a roaring fire, and sipping our brandies."

Thomas returned the smile. "Very well." As he followed Tony, backtracking through the club to the grand foyer, he questioned himself. He knew with certainty he'd allow no one else to deflect questions as easily as he had Tony Brazzio. Why was that? What was it about the man that had Thomas feeling so easygoing, so relaxed?

Tony was handsome, yes, but Thomas had been in the company of handsome men before. Why did this one make him want to forget he was a detective, and simply remember he was a man—a man with needs, with desires. Who appreciated a strong jaw and a brilliantly white smile, and dark eyes that glittered when amused.

Was that it? Was his physical attraction to Tony interfering with his effectiveness as a detective? Should it matter? Didn't he deserve some time to enjoy himself? Then he remembered who'd sent him to Club Raven and why, and decided he needed that brandy more than ever.

Chapter Ten

Quite possibly the largest, most ferocious-looking man in Baltimore stood sentry on the second-floor landing. His skin was so dark it gleamed blue in the lamplight, and his teeth, while brilliantly white, were filed into wicked points. He wore nothing but an animal skin—it was spotted today, Tony noticed, cheetah perhaps—wrapped around his hips, leaving his powerful torso and heavily muscled legs and arms bare except for gleaming golden rings encircling his biceps, wrists, and ankles.

Tony wasn't at all surprised when Thomas froze in his tracks, one hand slipping underneath his coat jacket, and immediately guessed what Thomas was reaching for. It stood to reason a detective would be armed.

Tony placed a reassuring hand on his arm. "Everything is fine, Detective. This is Kwanele, our house protector, for lack of a better term. He guards the more private areas of Club Raven from intruders. Kwanele, this is Detective Clare. He's my guest."

Kwanele's expression remained impassive. "This man, he has a good heart, but he means ill toward your guests with the funny accents."

Thomas shook his head. "I harbor no ill will toward anyone."

Tony smiled at him. "I'm afraid Kwanele is rather talented at ferreting out those who mean us harm, but in your case, I don't think there's cause for alarm." He looked at Kwanele. "I will vouch for him. He won't harm Bull and Dandy."

He didn't miss Thomas's eyes growing wide at the mention

of Bull and Dandy's names, but he wasn't surprised, either. He knew from the moment he heard Clare's name why Clare was at Club Raven's door, and who he wanted to see.

Clare was there for Bull and Dandy. Tony supposed he should've never let Clare inside, let alone offered him brandy to be taken in Tony's private suite, or given him a tour of the club. He should've ordered Clare from the property.

But there was something about Clare that sparked Tony's interest. It wasn't sexual appeal. Clare was a good-looking man, attractive perhaps, but not overly handsome, and while he sported a luxurious handlebar mustache, he wasn't the sort of man Tony usually lusted after. Clare was tall and broad-shouldered, while Tony favored smaller, more slender men. But Tony could tell there was a keen mind at work behind Clare's blue eyes, and therein lay the rub.

It'd been so long since Tony had a conversation with someone other than club members that he ached for the opportunity. He wanted to hear opinions different from those held by the men who frequented Club Raven. Thoughts on politics, on the Reconstruction, on the railroad, even on the new monument erected on Edgar Allan Poe's grave. He craved hear of other cities, other places, and even Baltimore as seen through someone else's experiences.

More importantly and less selfishly, he needed to figure out a way to get Clare to help him find out if anyone other than the mayor wanted to hurt Bull and Dandy. He needed Clare cemented on his side, and fully loyal to his cause.

Kwanele nodded, and moved aside so they could pass.

He led Clare up the second flight of stairs, hoping they would lead to the second-floor landing. Sometimes, they didn't. The stairways and halls in Club Raven had a strange way of moving around, as if trying to confuse people, the owners included. Just as the paintings hanging on the walls would sometimes change. The pastoral scene you'd admired in the dining room at breakfast would suddenly change to an impressionist still life by lunch.

Of course, the members thought it was just the owners having a bit of fun at their expense, but Tony, Matthias, and Julian knew the truth.

Club Raven was haunted.

More than that, the club was built on a nexus, an intersection of power where the veil between this world and all others was the thinnest. At Club Raven, the supernatural was a part of life. Indeed, many of their servants were ghosts, including Walther, who'd once confided in Tony that he'd died in 1861, the house slave of a man who owned a glue factory.

Not that he felt obligated to share any of this with Detective Clare. He knew how hard it would be for someone from the outside to put faith in the power of the house or the supernatural origins of many of its residents, and had no wish for Clare to think him mad.

Thankfully, he didn't need to broach the subject. The second floor behaved itself, as did the third and fourth floor staircases, and they arrived at his apartment without incident. He let them in, allowing Clare to precede him.

Clare was gaping at the grandeur of the apartment, his head swiveling on his neck as he took in the ceiling-to-floor windows, the golden damask drapery, the fine, European furniture, and thick Persian rugs. Tony bit back a grin, and gestured toward the marble fireplace. A fire had indeed been lit, and the room was toasty warm. "Shall we sit?"

Walther waited patiently next to the pair of armchairs clustered near the fireplace. He held two delicate snifters of amber liquid.

Clare jerked in surprise. "I...I didn't see him when I walked in."

"Oh? Isn't that odd," Tony replied. *Probably because he wasn't there until now. Ghosts have a way of popping in and out of rooms at will.* "Please, make yourself comfortable." He took a seat on one of the chairs, and accepted a glass from Walther.

Clare sat and took his glass as well. "Thank you."

Walther bowed. "My pleasure, sir. Will there be anything else?"

Tony shook his head. "No, Walther. Not now. I'll ring for you if we need anything."

"Yes, sir."

Walther walked away, and Tony knew if either he or Clare had been watching, Walther would've used the door to exit the room, but since neither one was paying him any attentionhe probably just melted away into thin air.

They chatted a while about what most people would consider mundane things—the weather, the Reconstruction, the current state of Baltimore's economy. Idle chitchat that would probably bore anyone else half to death, but lifted Tony's spirits considerably.

Thomas Clare possessed a very firm belief system, solid values, and had an opinion, it seemed, about everything. Although he agreed with less than half of them, Tony enjoyed hearing about them.

They sipped the fine brandy and watched the dancing flames, and laughed about observed singularities or banalities of fellow Baltimore citizens, or argued good-naturedly over differences in political views. Whenever their glasses neared empty, Walther would unobtrusively appear at their elbow with a bottle to refill them. Ghosts were good at that, too.

It was a more than pleasant way to pass an evening, but Tony reminded himself he couldn't waste the opportunity by doing nothing but getting drunk with Detective Thomas Arthur Clare, as much as he would've liked to just that. By previous arrangement with Walther, the bottle used to refill Thomas's glass was the finest brandy the club had to offer, but his own glass was filled with nothing but strong tea.

When Thomas's speech began to slur and his head began to bob, Tony knew the time was right. He set his glass on a table next to his chair and got up, then knelt between Thomas's knees. As tempting as the thought was, he ignored the significant bulge at Thomas's crotch and tried to make eye contact. "Thomas? Thomas, can you hear me?"

"Of coursh I can hear you. Drunk, not deaf."

Tony chuckled and nodded. "Of course. Tell me, Thomas, what do you want most? What's your most secret desire?"

Thomas waved a hand at him, liquid sloshing in his glass. "Nothing. I'm fine. More brandy, maybe."

"Yes, yes, Walther will fill that glass up in a moment, but surely there's something you want, something you haven't been able to secure for yourself? Tell me what it is." He used his power to give Thomas a nudge.

Thomas looked to the left and right as if to make sure nobody was listening—although Tony was fairly certain he couldn't see anything past the end of his nose very clearly. "Sex." He giggled like a schoolboy.

"Sex? What sort of sex, Thomas? You're a good-looking man. Surely you have no trouble securing like-minded coquettes?"

He giggled again. "No, no. Man sex. He put his glass between his knees and mimicked anal sex by repeatedly pushing a forefinger through a hole formed by making a loose fist with his other hand. The liquid in his glass slopped over the rim and made a wet spot on his thigh.

Tony gently removed the glass from between Thomas's knees and put it back in Thomas's hand. "Ah, I understand completely. Anything else? Something you might be too embarrassed to ask anyone about, or something that's too dirty to speak aloud?"

Thomas took another long swallow of liquor, and bobbed his head. "You won't tell anyone?"

"Of course not. We're friends, aren't we?"

"Yesh, Friends." He looked around the room again, then offered Tony a wide, sheepish grin. "I want to get spanked."

Tony's eyebrows shot up as if trying to jump off his forehead. "Spanked? You mean...?" He pantomimed spanking with the flat of his hand.

"Yesh, yesh!" Thomas nodded vigorously, the liquid in his glass splashing all over. "I've been a bad boy. I want to be punished. Then, you know...fucked."

Tony sat back on his haunches. This was a development he hadn't seen coming, but definitely one he could use to his advantage. "All right, then." He stood up, and pulled over an ottoman. Picking up Thomas's feet, he rested them on the upholstered stool, then took Thomas's glass once it was emptied. "Why don't you rest here for a while? I'll be right back." He gave another little push with his power.

"I'm gonna take a nap," Thomas muttered. His eyelid fluttered, then drifted closed, his chin lowering to touch his chest. Within moments, he began to snore softly.

"Walther?"

Walther appeared immediately, holding a brandy bottle. "More for the detective, sir?"

"No, he's out cold. He'll stay out, too, until I get things set up. Run and fetch one of the errand boys from downstairs, will you? I must send a message to Maude Breem. I need to ask a favor of her."

Thomas became aware of three things almost simultaneously. First, the light in the room, although soft and golden, cast from gas lamps, sliced into his eyes like butcher knives. He remembered drinking with Tony, but must've imbibed far more than he thought.

The second thing was that he was completely naked.

And thirdly, he couldn't decide which of the first two was the more vexing.

"Goddamn it!" He cast about the room, frantic to either find something with which to cover himself, or at least discover the person responsible for him being sans clothing. Neither seemed readily available. "Tony? Walther? Where the fuck has everyone gone?"

He wasn't even sure what room he was in. Not one Tony had showed him earlier, for sure. This room was...well, he didn't know what it was supposed to be, really. Because of the presence of a large featherbed, a desk, and a chair, one might assume it to be a boudoir, but there was an odd, X-shaped wooden cross against one wall, a barrel lying on its side and wrapped in rope, and shackles dangling from the ceiling. He didn't know what to make of it.

He strode across the room to the door and tried twisting the knob, but it was locked. He pounded on it with his fist but the door was solid and well-made, and absorbed his most powerful blows. "Hello? Brazzio? Hello! Somebody open this fucking door! I will fucking arrest everyone in this building, I swear it!"

"You have a quite a temper."

He froze but recovered quickly, spinning around at the sound of the masculine voice. His hand went to slip under his jacket to get to his revolver, but met only skin. *Oh, yes. Naked.* He cupped his privates instead. "Who are you?"

The man facing him looked older than Thomas by several years, and was dressed in a most peculiar fashion, wearing only a pair of snug-fitting black breeches that were tight enough as to leave little to the imagination. Or rather, were tight enough to fuel Thomas's imagination quite nicely. He was quite muscular, and his broad, bare chest was dusted with dark hair. He was also attractive, given his high cheekbones and a strong, well-defined jaw, along with dark, piercing eyes and full, sculpted lips.

Indeed, he was a fine a specimen of man as Thomas had seen in quite some time, and never had seen while wearing quite so little. His cock stiffened under his cupped hands despite the oddness of the situation in which he found himself.

"My name is inconsequential. You shall call me 'Sir.'"

"Sir...what? You don't sound British."

Those full lips slanted in a smile that sent a shiver up Thomas's back. "While I appreciate your wit, your backside will pay for your attempts at humor. I am just Sir." The man walked toward him, tapping a long, flexible cane against his palm. "You I shall call by your given name. Thomas, is it?"

"Y-yes, I'm Thomas. Now, see here, what are you playing at?" He took a step back from the peculiar stranger who called himself by an honorific. "I am a detective with the Baltimore Police Department and I—"

Sir whacked the cane against his palm, and Thomas's voice cut off as if sliced by a knife. Beneath his cupped hands, his cock was hard and aching. "Not in here. In this room, you are a terribly wicked young man who must be punished."

Those words sent a bolt of desire directly into Thomas's balls. How had this man known his secret fantasy? A fuzzy memory of him discussing taboo subjects with Tony while tossing back brandies dancing tauntingly in his mind. Had Tony set this up? Was this man being paid to be here? Of course! Why else would a stranger happen to show up in a locked room with Thomas—who was conveniently naked—and speak the very words Thomas fantasized about late at night, alone in his room?

"I...I am. Very wicked."

"Indeed." Sir smiled, showing beautifully white teeth. "How would you like to be punished? I feel magnanimous today, and shall give you the choice. Caning over the barrel? Whipping on the cross? Or perhaps a good, old-fashioned spanking with you bent over my knee?"

The thought of the man's large hand connecting with the delicate flesh of Thomas's backside drew a drop of moisture from the tip of his cock. "Yes, I think as spanking is in order."

"Sir. Say it." Sir's tone would not be disobeyed.

"A spanking, Sir."

"Very well." Sir walked over to the desk and pulled out the chair. He sat down, and placed the cane on the desk. Patting his knee, he motioned for Thomas to approach. "Come here."

Thomas walked over to where Sir sat, his knees trembling— not from fear, but from excitement. He stood in front of Sir, uncertain of how to proceed. He knew what would happen next in his fantasies, but was out of his element about how it would play out in real life.

He needn't have worried. Sir knew exactly what to do. "Bend over and rest your stomach on my lap."

Thomas lowered himself to lay across Sir's knees, but his cheeks burned brightly as he did so, because the act necessitated removing his cupped hands from his privates. His cock, full and reddened, sprang into view. It pressed against Sir's leg, sending shivers of pleasure through Thomas. He wanted to rub himself against Sir like an alley cat, but thought better of it. He didn't think Sir would appreciate such wantonness.

He gasped when he felt Sir's hand smooth over his ass. No one had ever touched him this way. The few times he'd managed to find like-minded men for sex, it had been quick, dirty, and over far sooner than he would've liked. An eager mouth sucking his cock in an alley, or the extremely rare, well paid whore bend-ing over for him in a cathouse somewhere far from Baltimore comprised the extent of his experience.

"You've been wicked." Sir's hand suddenly slammed down on Thomas's ass, drawing a spontaneous yelp from Thomas. "Very wicked, indeed. Swearing. Pounding on the door. You should be ashamed of yourself!" That lovely, calloused hand struck again and again, until Thomas began wiggling on Sir's lap. Then it would stop and gently massage the bruised flesh, almost tenderly rubbing the sting away. "You have a lovely ass. So very nice and round."

Thomas mewled, absurdly grateful for Sir's compliment. He wanted Sir to appreciate his body, to want it, to want him. He wanted to please Sir, with his mouth, with his ass. He'd never been breached, but it was his secret dream to be taken, to let go of all control, to be ridden until his seed spilled. He wondered if Sir knew this, too, and would act on it.

He sincerely hoped Sir would.

Then all thoughts were smacked away as Sir delivered a new set of spanks to Thomas's already tender buttocks. Again, the punishment stopped, and a comforting hand massaged the hurt away. He gasped when Sir parted his ass cheeks, exposing his hole to the cool air.

"Lovely. Just lovely. I'll bet that naughty ass is tight. Is it, Thomas? Is it tight?" A fingertip touched the wrinkled flesh, just barely pushing in. "It feels as if it is. But do you deserve my cock? I think not. You've not done anything to merit it yet." He gave Thomas's ass cheek a pinch, and then ordered Thomas to stand. "Get up."

Thomas rose to his needs immediately, eager to please. His legs shook and his ass burned, but his cock was harder than ever. The head was wet, precome slicking it. He wanted to touch himself, to bring himself to completion, but knew Sir would not allow it.

How easy it was to slip into this character, this person who wanted to obey, to be ordered, to be punished. So unlike Thomas, and yet touching a part of him deep inside that he kept hidden, making him feel a relief from a burden he hadn't even been aware he'd been carrying!

There was no more time for introspection. Sir ordered him to the barrel.

It was a wine barrel at one time. The perfume of good wine still clung to it, flooding Thomas's mouth with the memory of the taste of fine French vintage. Sir told him to bend over the barrel, much as he had over Sir's lap.

This was different, though. Sir used chains to bind Thomas to the barrel, securing his arms and legs, tethering him in place. What was Sir going to do that necessitated Thomas being bound? For a moment, true fear stabbed his heart, and he found it difficult to breathe.

"Easy, Thomas. Breathe." Sir comforted him, rubbing his back. He felt the gentle press of soft lips to his skin, and the warmth of Sir's breath as Sir lay a trail of kisses along Thomas's spine. "There. See? All is well. You must learn to give all control over to me. Only then will you soar."

Yes, that sounds good. I want that, whatever "soaring" means. He felt the need for it deep in his bones. Thomas took in a few deep, calming breaths, and felt the tension slip from his muscles.

"That's much better. Are you ready?"

"Yes." Although what he was agreeing to, he didn't know. He was shocked to find he already trusted Sir, even though he had no idea who the man really was. It didn't matter. It was Sir, and Sir would take care of him.

He howled when the cane struck his ass the first time, more out of surprise than pain. Oh, the pain was there, make no mistake. It felt diamond bright and razor sharp, but there was pleasure in it, too, so equally cutting that he couldn't quite distinguish between the two. His cock flagged, but his balls swelled, as if his body was confused.

The second strike of the cane made him arch off the barrel, although the ropes kept him from jumping free. By the fifth blow he was yelping, but his erection had returned. The hits blurred one into another and his mind grew fuzzy, suddenly unable to think in words. He felt as if he were floating, was somehow disconnected from his body, from the pain, from the pleasure, from everything.

He soared.

Chapter Eleven

There was no telling how much time passed. Perhaps Thomas had blacked out, but the last thing he remembered was Sir draping him over the barrel. He now lay on the featherbed, stretched out on his stomach. Reaching around, he gently touched his rear end, feeling welts crisscrossing the flesh. Hissing, he pulled his hand away.

Sir stood next to the bed, naked, having removed his breeches at some point, although Thomas had no recollection of when. "Sore? You should be. I'm told this was your first time, but you took quite a beating. I don't usually cane someone on the first visit, but somehow I knew you needed it."

Thomas didn't reply. He didn't know what to say. *Yes, I needed you to beat the shit out of me* didn't quite seem something one grown man should say to another, even though he believed on some level that was exactly what had happened.

"Well, are you ready?"

"For what?" He didn't think his ass could take another caning. He wouldn't be able to sit down for a week from the feel of things as it was.

Sir smiled. "To continue."

Oh, no. No, no, no! Thomas rolled to his side as if to hide his sore ass from Sir. "I think not."

Sir laughed. "No, you misunderstand." He fisted his cock, thick and pretty and already stiffening, and began to stroke it. "You want this, don't you? You have since you first woke up in the room and saw me."

Ah, that was different. That he could do. Thomas smiled. "Yes, Sir. I do want it. You have a handsome cock."

"As do you." Sir put one knee up on the bed, and angled his hips so his cock could reach Thomas's mouth. He brushed the head of his cock over Thomas's lips, precome wetting them. "Now, open that sweet mouth of yours and suck me."

He obeyed at once, opening his mouth and taking the head of Sir's cock in. He tasted brine and wanted more, sucking in Sir's length. His let it out again, letting his lips push the foreskin back, his tongue slide over the smooth head.

"Fuck! Yes, that's so good." Sir twisted his fingers in Thomas's hair, holding Thomas still. His hips thrust, feeding his length into Thomas's willing mouth.

Sir pushed in deep, until Thomas felt the cockhead hit the back of his throat, and curly pubic hair tickle his nose. He concentrated on not gagging, refusing to allow his body to reject any of Sir's saliva-slicked prick.

When Sir pulled away from him he growled, and was rewarded with a sharp slap on his already-scored buttocks. "Patience, patience. You'll do as I say, Thomas."

It was an effort to bend his will to Sir's again, especially since his body was aching with desire grown to a fever pitch. His cock stood at a sharp angel from his belly, hard and needing. When he spoke, it was through gritted teeth. "Yes, Sir."

Sir gave him a slanted smile, but his eyes sparkled with humor, and a desire that matched Thomas's own. "Get up on your hands and knees."

Thomas blinked at him. "What?"

"Your hands and knees. Now. Or do I need to teach you another lesson?"

Thomas was thunderstruck, and stared wide-eyed at Sir for a long moment, locked in a silent battle of wills. He knew what happened to men who assumed the position for other men.

He'd been on the giving end before, but... Hadn't he dreamed of pretending to be passive, of offering his ass to a more dominant man? Well, this was his chance, and suddenly a fresh needle of need stabbed him deep, propelling him up onto his hands and knees.

"Good boy."

He watched from over his shoulder as Sir climbed up onto the bed with him, and took up a position behind him. He shivered when Sir nudged his legs apart, and when a strong hand pushed his head down to the mattress.

He felt a little strange, kneeling on the bed with his ass up in the air, but then all concerns of how he might look vanished with the first prodding of Sir's spit-slicked cock at his hole. It pushed in slowly, so slowly, forcing its way past muscle that fought to keep it out.

A stinging slap on his ass cheek brought a grunt to his lips. "Relax. Concentrate on letting me in."

He did. It was difficult, and more than a little uncomfortable, but the more Sir slid into his body, the better it felt. When Sir was finally fully seated inside him and Thomas could feel the scratch of pubic hair against his sore ass, he felt oddly complete. Reaching between his legs, he began to stroke himself.

"That's it. Make it come for me. I want to smell it on the sheets," Sir said. He began to move, slow thrusts that seemed to hit a delicious spot deep inside that Thomas hadn't been aware existed.

Bolts of pleasure rushed through him, and he grit his teeth against the climax that exploded within him. He came, harder than he ever had before. Stars winked at the edge of his vision as his hot seed spotted the mattress beneath him.

Sir pulled out of his ass and, from the liquid heat Thomas felt on his back and ass, had come as well, perhaps even at the same time. The thought somehow made Thomas feel even better, and a little bit proud.

The best part, though, came when Sir stretched out full length on the bed, and pulled Thomas close. Their bodies spooned one another, fitting together as closely as those Russian nesting dolls Thomas had seen once in a fancy store up in New York.

He felt relaxed, at peace, as if the heavy burden of worry and tension that was a constant part of his life as a detective had vanished. He felt light, buoyant, and knew without a doubt it was all due to Sir.

What would happen when they left this room? Would he ever see Sir again? He didn't even know Sir's real name.

As if he read Thomas's mind, Sir shushed him. "Be still now, Thomas. Rest. We'll talk later, after you wake. For now, your body needs time to heal."

Once again, he obeyed Sir without question. His eyelids drifted closed, and he slept.

Tony reached for the small, soft towel he'd brought with him into the passageway behind the wall of the playroom, and wiped the semen from his hands and cock. Watching Thomas and Leopold—whom Thomas called "Sir"—from the eyes of the painting hanging across from the bed had been quite thrilling.

He liked secretly watching men having sex with other men almost as much as he enjoyed participating in the act. Voyeurism was his fetish, his secret passion, as much as getting spanked was Thomas's. He couldn't see the harm in indulging himself from time to time since it harmed no one, although he would much rather watch in plain view of the men who were fucking. He enjoyed being in the room with them, hearing the sounds, smelling the scents, but he couldn't pass up seeing what happened when Thomas got his most secret desire.

After he'd pulled his pants back up, he felt his way through the passage to the moveable bookcase in the study next to the playroom and pushed it. It slid open and he slipped into the study, then pushed it shut again. Looking at it, no one would suspect there was a passage behind it.

There were several such clandestine passages in Club Raven, and he knew and used them all. Except for when the club decided it didn't want someone sneaking around through its secret arteries and sealed them shut.

He'd once gotten trapped that way once, stuck between the walls with his dick in his hand, and had to yell for Walther to get someone to free him. Julian and Matthias never let him forget it, either.

Speaking of Walther, he appeared at Tony's side and reached for the towel. "Shall I fetch a plate of food for you to your suite, sir?"

A smile tilted his lips. "Actually, yes. It seems I've worked up quite an appetite. Bring me some of that cold chicken Mama put up, and a pot of tea, will you?"

"Very good, sir." Walther's voice faded away with the rest of him.

Good ol' Walther. He never questioned anything he saw, or breathed a word of any secrets he was privy to, not once in all the time Tony had known him. Unlike Mama—who never, *ever* broached the subject, but whom Tony was sure suspected—Walther *knew* about Tony's proclivities, but never judged him. He was lucky to have Walther as his manservant, ghost or no, and knew it.

He paused in front of the playroom door, making sure his shirt was tucked and his buttons were done up properly, then rapped his knuckles smartly on the wood. He didn't wait for an answer before stepping inside.

Thomas yelped and jumped out of the bed, tugging the sheet

with him. He wrapped it around his hips as if he could hide the fact he was stark naked.

Leopold, on the other hand, lounged languidly on the mattress, his legs spread and heavy cock lying soft against his thigh. He offered Tony a smile. "Good evening."

Tony nodded and grinned. "Looks like it was most definitely good, for some of us anyway." He nodded at Thomas, who was gaping at him. "Evening, Thomas. Enjoying yourself?"

"This...this isn't what it looks like." Thomas's face grew red, and he stammered. Quite adorable, actually, coming from the usually tough, hardened detective.

Tony chuckled. "Oh, that's sad. Because what it looks like to me is the two of you made good use of the Club Raven playroom."

"Playroom!" Thomas looked so startled by the idea he nearly dropped the sheet and had to fumble to keep it up around his waist. "You mean other people...the cross and the barrel and..."

"Of course! Why, surely you didn't think you were the only one!" Tony clucked his tongue at Thomas. "After our talk last night, I thought it would be a gesture of goodwill to introduce you to Leopold, one of the most popular Dominants in Baltimore."

"I thank you for the introduction, by the way," Leopold said. He reached over and tugged the sheet off Thomas's hips. Tony noticed Thomas gasped and glared, but one look from Leopold stayed Thomas's hand from reaching for the sheet again. He also noticed when Thomas half-turned toward Leopold that Thomas's ass had been scored with a lovely crosshatch pattern.

"Beautiful work, Leopold." Tony walked closer to get a better look.

"I think he enjoyed it. I know I did," Leopold replied. He cupped Thomas's butt cheek in appeared to be a possessive manner. He noticed Thomas didn't pull away from Leopold's touch, either.

Good, Tony thought. *There's a real connection between them.*

Thomas looked as if he wished the floor of the club would open and swallow him down whole. He lifted his chin and leveled a stoic look at Tony. "I suppose this means you'll be reporting me to Captain More."

Tony cocked his head. "Report you? For what?"

"For this. Being a homosexual and...you know..." He gestured toward the equipment in the room. "Behavior unbecoming a duly appointed officer of the law."

Tony and Leopold exchanged bemused glances, then both burst into laughter. "My dear Thomas, if I reported every man who indulged his individual desires at Club Raven, we'd have no members left except for the few old dodgers downstairs! Even we owners would be in jail. Have no fear, my friend. You're free to be yourself here without worry or judgment."

Thomas looked from Tony to Leopold and back again, and Tony saw the glimmer of tears in his eyes. "That is very kind of you, but I'm not a member, nor do I foresee becoming one on my salary. I thank you for last evening, though, and for tonight."

A satisfied smile played at Tony's lips. "Well, we at Club Raven would be more than happy to gift you with a membership."

"You mean a bribe, sir?" Thomas straightened, his gaze suddenly grown cold.

"Nonsense. A bribe is an ugly word for an ugly arrangement. This is simply a gift from one friend to another."

Thomas didn't look convinced. He folded his arms across his chest, although it didn't have as much impact as he may have hoped since he was still naked. "And what do you want from me?"

Tony rolled his eyes. "Fine. The two men you came here looking for, Bull and Dandy? I want them left alone. They haven't done anything. Indeed, it's because they caught your boss, Mayor Forge, in a compromising position at the Soiled

Dove that you've been sent after them."

To Tony's surprise, instead of appearing shocked, Thomas laughed. "Is that all? I already know Forge was at Maude Breem's place. He's a frequent customer, from my understanding." He offered up a wry grin. "I came here under the pretense of looking for Bull and Dandy, but I really just wanted a look inside Club Raven. I'd heard rumors, you see...although the truth surpasses any rumor I ever heard."

He yelped when Leopold swatted his behind. "You naughty boy!"

"Later, Leopold. I want to hear what he has to say, first." Tony waggled a finger at him, although he couldn't help smiling. This was turning out better than he'd ever hoped.

"At first Forge told me he wanted Bull and Dandy dead, but I flat-out refused. Who kills someone over a stolen pocket watch? I knew Forge was holding vital information back. When I finally got him to tell me why he wanted them so badly, I realized that if I brought them back, he would kill them. It's the only way he can be sure they won't talk."

Tony sighed and nodded. "I believe you're right. He *will* kill them, and what's more, he won't stop hunting for them until he finds them." He looked at Thomas. "Would you be willing to do us a favor? Mind you, whether you agree or not, the membership at Club Raven is yours for the asking. This is above and separate from that, a personal favor to me."

"What is it?"

"I need to get in to see Forge, and I need to be alone with him for a few minutes." He held up a hand before Thomas could speak. "I'm not going to hurt him. I just need a bit of time to convince him it's not in his best interest to continue looking for Bull and Dandy."

Thomas shook his head. "I know Forge, and he won't be deterred so easily."

"Let's just say I have a way with words, shall we?" Tony smirked. "It won't hurt to let me talk to him, will it?"

Thomas looked down at Leopold, who shrugged. "You need to do what you think best, Thomas."

He chewed on his bottom lip for a moment, staring at Tony as if trying to read Tony's thoughts. "A couple of conditions, first. You're not to carry a weapon into the mayor's office, nor will you lock the door. I'll stand directly outside it, ready to rush in should the mayor call for me. Understand this—I am an officer of the law. If you attempt to do bodily harm to Forge, I will shoot you."

"Agreed." Tony nodded and smiled. "I just want to talk to him."

"Very well, then. I think it's a waste of your time, but I'll arrange a meeting tomorrow." He paused for a heartbeat or two, then added, "And I'd very much like to take you up on your generous offer of membership into your fine club."

Tony chuckled when Leopold suddenly reached up and grabbed Thomas around the waist and toppled him into bed. "Right, then. Looks like you boys will be able to amuse yourselves for the time being without me."

He was still laughing long after he'd left, the sounds of Leopold's hand smacking Thomas's bottom ringing in his ears.

Chapter Twelve

Bull sat at a table in Tony's apartment, a smirk lifting one of his cheeks as he watched Dandy be fitted for his suit. A tailor was on his knees, measuring Dandy's inseam, and Dandy's face was nearly crimson with embarrassment. "Aw, why are you looking so offended? It ain't the first time a man played billiards with your balls."

"Aw, just you wait, Bull. It's your turn next, and see how you like this wrinkle up old man fondling your jewels."

"Please, sir, stand still!" The tailor, an Englishman who'd made all of Tony's suits, turned toward Tony for help. "Sir, please, I can't get a proper measurement if he keeps moving about."

"All right, all right. Dandy, hold still or I'll nail your feet to the floor. Let Chester get your measurements. You, Bull, stop egging him on."

Dandy frowned, but held still, at least for a few minutes. "I don't understand why we need fancy duds like this. It's a waste of money, ain't it?"

"No, it isn't," Tony said for what felt like the hundredth time. "You promised to do as I asked if I helped you. I've held up my end of the agreement—I've got Detective Clare to quit chasing you, and I'm going to convince Forge to leave you alone. Now it's your turn. I need to turn you two street rats into gentlemen, and the first step in doing that is to dress you properly."

Bull made a rude noise. "Bah. You can't take a rat and call it a swan. It's still just a rat, only dressed in better fur."

"I agree. It'll take more than just dressing you up, but that's the first step." Tony reached over for a small, silver bell he kept on the buffet near the table and rang it. It made a delicate musical sound that was almost insubstantial; still, it did as it was intended and summoned Walther. "We'll take tea in the other room, Walther."

Walther gave him a short bow. "As you wish, sir."

"I don't drink tea. Can't stand the stuff," Bull said. He wrinkled his nose and lip at the same time.

Tony held up his hand. "The tea isn't what's important. You don't need to like it, but you'll learn how to drink it. Every fine gentleman knows how, and you'll learn just as I did, like it or not. You'll also learn how to appreciate fine wine and spirits, and an expensive cigar. I also want you to take elocution lessons."

"Oh, no!" Dandy stepped away from the tailor. "That's the end of it all, bucko. I heard about that elocution stuff back in Five Points. Invisible stuff supposed to give off light like magic. Bah! I don't trust what I can't see."

Bull gave his head a vigorous nod. "I agree, boyo. Ain't gonna get no elocution on me, neither."

Tony smirked at the two of them. "This is exactly what I mean—you need to be educated. I learned, and you'll learn, too. Elocution means the way people talk. You're thinking of electricity. New fangled thingamabob. I heard some fellow just patented a special glass blub for it."

The tailor sighed and held up his measuring tape. "Please, sir, may we continue? It'll be dark soon, and I've promised the missus I'll be home in time for supper."

"Of course, Chester. Bull, it's your turn." Tony crooked his finger at Bull.

"Might as well get it over and done with, boyo." Dandy sat down and scratched his belly. "He'll go on about it all night if you don't let this fella measure your sac."

"I am not measuring..." The tailor looked at Tony in exasperation. "Please, sir! Explain to them that I am not molesting them!"

"Let it go, Dandy. You, too, Bull." Tony gave them each a hard stare, and although they rolled their eyes, they fell silent. Chester was able to finish up his work relatively quickly, gathered up his tapes, notebook, and samples, and left after a short, quick bow.

Tony sighed. If something as simple as getting Bull and Dandy measured for new suits was as vexing as it had been, he couldn't imagine how hard the other lessons were going to go, and questioned whether it would be worth the trouble.

Then he looked at Bull and Dandy and once again saw himself in their place. He took a deep breath, said a silent prayer for strength and patience, and said, "All right, time for tea. Follow me."

Forge did not seem to be in a very good mood when Thomas escorted Tony into his office. His florid face looked redder than usual, and his eyes were narrowed and cold. He looked up with surprise when they walked into the room, but his demeanor changed quickly and he glowered at them. "What do you want? I'm a very busy man. I haven't time to meet privately with citizens without an appointment. I must insist you—"

"Mayor Forge, we *do* have an appointment." Thomas gestured to Tony. "Mr. Brazzio has, I mean. I arranged it with your assistant yesterday."

He didn't seem convinced. "Impossible. I wasn't informed of any meeting. Jenkins!" He looked toward the open door. "Jenkins! Come in here at once!"

Thomas held up a hand. "He's gone on his dinner break, Mayor."

"How very convenient. You claim to have an appointment, and he's gone off for supper." Forge didn't bother trying to cover his scowl or his obvious distaste for Tony. "You're Mr. Bravo from Club Raven, aren't you?"

"Brazzio, sir, and yes, I am. I have an important matter to discuss privately with you."

"I assume you are here to talk about those two miscreants, the Irishmen I sent Detective Clare to find." He cast a black look at Thomas. "I have no idea why he's brought you here and not them, but I am not in the habit of meeting with men of your... character, privately or otherwise."

It was Tony's turn to scowl. "I beg your pardon? What are you insinuating?"

"Simply that, from what I've been told, you're an ill-bred hoodlum from the streets of New York, not a genteel man of breeding and means. You're only a partial owner of the club, aren't you? Whatever pressing matter you wish to discuss would be better served if one of your betters came to speak with me about it. Sophisticated men hold discussions in this office, not uneducated hooligans."

Tony felt tension tightened his muscles, and he wanted nothing more than to jump over Forge's desk and plow his fist into Forge's doughy face. He resisted, but only barely and with great difficulty. "I assure you, I am possessed of adequate intelligence, and more than well suited to discuss this particular matter."

"I believe it would be in your best interest to consent to this conversation, Mayor Forge." Thomas's jaw looked carved from granite, and Tony could practically feel the steel in his gaze. Forge didn't seem to miss the meaning in it, either.

"Are you threatening me, Detective?"

"Yes, actually. I am. I'm going to leave this office now, and you're going to suffer a conversation with Mr. Brazzio."

"I'll have your badge for this!"

Thomas's mouth slanted in a sardonic grin. "We'll see about that later, after your meeting is concluded." He turned to Tony and tipped his hat. "Mr. Brazzio, I'll be right outside should you need me." He glanced back at Fargo. "Or my gun."

Tony nodded at him. "That won't be necessary. Thank you, Thomas."

"My pleasure, Tony."

Their familiar use of first names didn't seem lost on Forge. His face grew even redder, and he heaved himself to his feet, bracing his hands on the desktop. "So, I was correct to surmise there is something going on here, some collusion between the two of you! What is it? What are you about?"

Neither of them answered. Instead, Thomas turned his back and left, closing the office door quietly behind him.

Tony turned his attention to Forge. He approached Forge's desk uninvited, trying to maintain eye contact with Forge. "Mr. Forge, we need to have a talk. You've been chasing two Irishmen, Bull and Dandy. You've accused them of stealing a pocket watch from you."

Forge jerked his head, as if to try to break the connection Tony had established, but failed. "That's right, they did. A gold one. They're thieves and the law demands they be punished. I can't have hoodlums like that running around the streets of my city."

Tony pushed with his power. "Listen to me very carefully. Bull and Dandy didn't not take your watch. You lost it, and they found it and returned it to you."

"No, they...no, it was..." Confusion colored his features, but he wasn't yet convinced. Tony pushed harder.

"You lost it, they found it, and gave it back. Where is the pocket watch now, Mayor Forge?"

"It's, it's in my wall safe, hidden behind that painting." Forge pointed to a framed pastoral painting hanging on the wall to the right of his desk.

"See? You have it because they returned it to you. Don't you remember?"

Forge nodded, slowly and unsure of himself. "Yes, yes, I think so. They gave it back to me. I thanked them?"

"Yes, you did. You were very gracious."

"Of course, I was. They were honest men who brought my property back to me." Forge began to relax, telling Tony his mind was accepting Tony's version of events as truth.

"Excellent." He gave Forge another small push with his power, just to cement the idea in Forge's head. "Thank you so much, Mayor Forge. You've been most helpful. I fear I must take my leave, though. I'm planning a party for Club Raven members, you see, and I'm terribly busy. Good day, sir."

"Very good of you to stop by. I'm glad to be of service." Forge sat down, and stared absently at his blotter. It would take another few minutes for the effect of Tony's power to fade, leaving Forge relaxed and content, and fully convinced the idea Tony planted was entirely his own.

Tony slipped out of the office and closed the door, then nodded to Thomas. "It's done."

"And that's it? He won't want me to bring Dandy and Bull in anymore?"

"He won't even understand why you're chasing them in the first place." Tony chuckled. "He thinks they're heroes, that he lost the pocket watch and they returned it to him."

"That is an amazing talent you have, Tony."

"All the better to serve club members with, Thomas."

They exchanged a grin and left City Hall, content their mission had been accomplished and neither would have any trouble from Mayor Forge again.

Chapter Thirteen

I'm sick to death of these lessons, Dandy. How to talk, how to walk, what fucking fork to use at supper! I've been feeding myself since before I wore short pants! Why do rich fucks need so many forks, anyway? Everybody only has one mouth, right?" He sat on the bed in their room, hands clenched together between his knees.

"Right you are, boyo." Dandy sat on a chair next to the bed. He plucked at the lapel of the new coat he wore. "These clothes are good and all, but me old clothes kept me just as warm and these brand new pockets are just as empty. Know what I keep thinking about? All those fat wallets downstairs in the Great Room." He kicked an ottoman, sending it sliding across the floor. "Why should we put on airs for Mr. Tony Brazzio? What's it going to get us?"

Bull nodded. "Exactly, what do we stand to gain? Nothing, I say. He gets to win his bet, or whatever the fuck it is he's after, and then what? He'll kick us out, that's what. Leave us to rot in the gutter, just like everybody else has."

"So, what do we do?"

"I don't know about you, boyo, I'm done with lessons. I'm going to go downstairs, fill my pockets with whatever I can steal, and leave this fucking place." Bull stood up and held out a hand to Dandy. "Are you going to join me, or are you going to stay here like some fucking doll Tony can dress up and show off?"

Dandy jumped up and grabbed Bull's hand. "I'm with you, boyo!"

They grinned at each other and then left their room, making their way downstairs. The hallway changed twice on the way, once leading them to Tony's suite—the last place they wanted to go—and once to the wickedly appointed "playroom," which they wanted to experiment in but hadn't yet had the opportunity. Now, they probably never would, but it was a small price to pay in Bull's opinion.

The third time was the charm as the hallway led them to the stairway, which obediently stayed in place and let them descend to the second floor. There Kwanele, the Zulu warrior who protected the upper floors of the club from unwanted visitors, stopped them.

"Going?" He grinned a mouthful of sharpened teeth at them.

"Yeah. Down to the dining hall." To Bull's credit, he didn't stammer, although his knees felt a little weak whenever he had to face Kwanele.

"Lie." The grin faded a bit, becoming more of a grimace.

Damn it all to Hell. He'd forgotten Kwanele's talent was ferreting out truth from lie, and knowing when someone was plotting against club members.

In other words, exactly what Bull and Dandy were planning to do.

"Fine. We're going to the Great Room, but we're not going to touch anybody." That was the truth—at least mostly. They were going to the Great Room, and they weren't going to actually, physically touch anyone. Bull would just use his power to lift the billfolds from the members' pockets into theirs.

Kwanele must've been able to sense it. From his expression, he wasn't completely satisfied, but couldn't find reason enough to hold them. He nodded, his expression still dark.

They hurried past Kwanele, and down the stairs to the first floor. Once in the foyer, Bull grabbed Dandy's arm and pulled him close enough to whisper in his ear. "We best be quick about our business, boyo. Kwanele is likely still suspect, and he'll mouth off to Tony about it as sure as the coat's on your back."

Dandy nodded and hastened his step, and led the way into the Great Room. It was fairly busy tonight, being a Friday, full of men who'd worked the week in their offices and were now ready to begin the week's end with a fine cigar and a glass of sherry.

While Tony had kept Dandy and Bull fairly secluded over the past few weeks while they labored with their lessons, most of the men in the Great Room paid them little mind. Unlike the first time they'd come to Club Raven, this time the clothes they wore were top-notch, finely tailored and fashioned of fine wool and linen. Their hair was neatly trimmed, and their nails, which Tony inspected every morning, were clean. They looked like they could be the sons of any one of the rich men in the room, young men of excellent breeding and bright futures, and as such passed as nearly invisible to the powerful men relaxing and puffing on fine cigars. They looked as though they belonged, so no one took the slightest notice of them.

None that is, except for one pair of blue eyes. Neither Bull nor Dandy noticed Thomas Clare standing in the far corner of the room sipping a glass of ruby red claret, but he spotted them immediately. His gaze never left them, following them as they moved about the room.

They developed a routine. Dandy would touch a man's shoulder or arm, and quickly discern the location of the man's billfold. Dandy would indicate the spot to Bull, who would use his power to lift the wallet from its owner and transport it into his own pocket. They worked the room quickly and efficiently, fleecing almost all the men present in nearly no time at all.

Bull and Dandy knew they couldn't return to their room since they'd need to pass Kwanele, and he would know immediately that they'd been up to no good regarding the members of the club. Instead, they left the Great Room and hurried across the foyer to the back service room, then out into the courtyard near the kitchen.

Following a path around the side of the kitchen, they entered a fence-enclosed garden. In summer it would be aflame with colorful flowers, and the air sweet with ripe fruit from several varieties of trees, but now it sat cold and barren, awaiting the first snowfalls of the year. No one was likely to come out there, and they thought they'd be undisturbed as they stripped the stolen billfolds of cash.

They would've been right, too, if it hadn't been for Thomas Clare.

"You there! What are you up to?" He marched into the garden, squaring off with Bull and Dandy.

Their hands were full of cash, and billfolds were scattered on the ground and on a wrought iron bench. Both of them swore and stuffed the money into their pockets, backing away from Clare. There was nowhere for them to go—they couldn't get out of the garden since Clare was blocking the only exit.

"Hey now, we ain't doing nothing." Bull straightened his spine and tried his best to look offended, even with stolen billfolds scattered about his feet.

"Nothing? You've robbed the members of the club!" Clare growled at them. "How could you do it, after all Tony's done for you? Look at you, wearing the clothes Tony had made for you. You ate at his table, and this is how you repay him? I should wring your scrawny necks!"

"What's it to you, anyway?" Dandy took a half step toward Clare. "We know who sent you here. You work for that slug, Forge! You don't give a fairy's fart about the members here."

Bull nodded. "And if you think you're bringing us back to Forge, you've got another think coming, boyo."

"I *used* to work for Forge. Now, I'm a full member of Club Raven, and I'll be damned if I'll stand by and watch a pair of plug-uglies steal their hard-earned money!"

"Hard earned!" Dandy barked a short, harsh laugh. "Those bastards never worked a day in their lives! Born with a silver spoon shoved up their asses, is what they are."

"Yeah," Bull said. "You want to see folks who work hard for every penny? Go up to Five Points. People there are poor as Job's turkey, gotta scratch for every penny they got. Those people in there don't know the meaning of the word *work*."

Clare scowled at them. "So, that means you can come in here and take what doesn't belong to you? Not while I'm around you can't. Empty your pockets immediately!" He took a couple of steps forward.

Bull and Dandy held their ground. Bull squeezed his hands into fists and put them up. This wouldn't be the first fight he was in, and as sure as cows had teats, wouldn't be his last. As far as he was concerned, the money was in his pocket which meant it belonged to him, and nobody, especially not highfaluting Detective Thomas Arthur Clare, was going to take it from him.

Clare put his fists ups as well, moving them slowly up and down in front of his face as he took a few steps closer. His gaze fixed on Bull, who danced lightly on his toes.

It was Dandy who threw the first punch. It came from the right, and landed on Clare's jaw, snapping Clare's head to the side.

One thing Clare might not know but would soon learn was that nobody fought fair on the streets of Five Points. They fought dirty, because to lose might just mean your death.

Before Clare could bounce back from the first blow, Bull threw a roundhouse that clocked him upside his skull. Clare's hair, so neatly combed a moment before, fell in disarray over his eyes.

Clare shook his head, then reached out and pushed Bull away. Turning, he managed to land a punch to Dandy's face. There was a cracking sound, and Bull saw blood gush from Dandy's nose.

Bull jumped on Clare's back, wrapping an arm around Clare's throat while leveling rapid blows to the side of his head. "You fucking broke Dandy's nose! I *liked* his nose!"

Dandy roared and tackled Clare's legs, bringing Clare down to the ground, and Bull with him. The three of them landed in a heap, arms and legs thrashing, fists pounding whatever bit of flesh they could reach. They rolled into the rosebushes, sharp thorns ripping through fabric and skin both. In short order, the three of them were bruises and bloodied, but none of them would give in and end the fight.

Walther had appeared in Tony's toilet at a most inconvenient time. "Walther! What have we discussed about a man's privacy?"

"They're fighting. Thought you might like to know." Walther didn't look concerned at all about Tony's obvious discomfort. Ghosts weren't typically shy about bodily functions, considering they no longer had any.

"Who's fighting?" Tony stood up and went about his business, trying to ignore the fact that he was being watched by a ghost. It wasn't easy, but he managed, mostly because he had no choice.

"The detective with the raw backside, and the two thieves. Sir, you really should think more carefully about who you allow into the club. These last three are making a nuisance of themselves."

Tony struggled to button his fly in the cramped space. "What happened? Do you know?"

Walther shrugged. "I believe the thieves stole, sir. From the members in the Great Room. Again."

Tony flinched at the reminder that Bull and Dandy had stolen from club members before. "And Clare?"

"He caught them out in the garden, stuffing their pockets with their ill-gotten goods, sir. He took offense, I should I think."

"I have no doubt he did." Tony rolled his eyes and pushed past Walther, stepping out of the water closet and into the hallway. He hurried to the stairs and followed them down past Kwanele, who arched a curious eyebrow at him, toward the main floor. Impatient to reach the bottom, he skipped the last few stairs by vaulting over the banister. He rushed through the service room and out into the courtyard.

He could hear the sound of scuffling coming from behind the kitchen and hurried around back. In the garden, he found Bull, Dandy, and Clare in a tangle of arms and legs, fists and feet flying. "Stop this! Stop this at once!" He grabbed the back of Clare's coat and pulled him up, using a foot to keep Bull from jumping up off the ground and pummeling Clare. A well-timed elbow caught Dandy in the ribs as he charged Clare.

It took a dose of Tony's power to get the three of them to finally stop fighting. He bent and scooped up a handful of scuffed and tattered billfolds. "You two! What do you have to say for yourselves?"

Dandy wiped a clot of blood from his nose. "You're not our keeper!"

"Nor our warden," Bull added. He pulled back his lips and jiggled a tooth that was loose.

"You're right. I'm not." He sent out a powerful push of his talent to Bull and Dandy. "You will return every fucking penny you stole to the members in the Great Room. You will tell them it was part of a college initiation—they'll understand and forgive that, providing they get their money back, and I salve their tempers with a few bottles of single malt. Then you'll go up to your room, pack your things, and get out of this club. I don't care where you go or what you do, but I never want to see your faces here again. If I do, I *will* let Detective Clare shoot you. Or better yet, I'll give you over to Kwanele. Now, go, get out of my sight."

Bull and Dandy blanched at the name of the Zulu warrior, and exchanged an uneasy glance. Although they'd talked tough about leaving, they hadn't expected Tony to actually throw them out. What were they going to do now? Especially since they had to return the money they'd taken and hadn't a legitimate penny saved between them?

Fighting Tony's suggestion to return their loot wasn't an option, and they knew it. By now they'd learned how powerful Tony's gift was, and how futile it was to try to fight it. Shoulders slumped in defeat, they picked up the billfolds and made their way back to the Great Room. Neither of them could meet Tony's eyes as they passed.

Chapter Fourteen

Tony stood in the dark passageway and flipped a small piece of hinged wood out of the way. He peered through the two holes the wood had concealed, looking out through the eyes of a portrait hanging in Bull and Dandy's room. He was interested in knowing what the two idiots were thinking, and what their plans were now that he'd essentially thrown them out of Club Raven.

They didn't have much to pack, just their old clothes and a few trinkets. All of it fit into the single, small valise they'd found in their room's massive wardrobe.

"What do you suppose we should do now? We don't even have the money to get back to Five Points." Dandy closed the lid of the suitcase and snapped the locks shut. He placed it on the floor and sat on the edge of the bed.

"Dunno," Bull said. He was sitting with his back resting against the headboard, one leg thrown up on the mattress. "Didn't think much past stealing the money and leaving before. Never thought we'd get caught."

"Yeah." Dandy chewed on his lip, as if mulling things over. "Think that's our problem, boyo?"

"What is?"

"Not thinking things through. Seems to me it's what gets us into the most trouble. We get an idea, and we're off and running. Except it don't usually work out the way we think."

Bull pursed his lips. "Maybe. How's that help our troubles now, though?"

"It don't. Just observin', is all."

They sat in silence for a long while. They weren't under a compulsion to leave as they had been to return the money to the club members. Tony hadn't used his power on them for that, and neither one seemed in any particularhurry to pick up the valise and leave Club Raven.

Tony figured they both knew they only one place to go after they left—the gutter. They'd lived there all their lives, and he couldn't imagine eitherwas anxious to go back.

Dandy seemed to arrive at the same conclusion. "Listen, Bull, you and me, we've been together since we were tots, yeah? Growing up hard in Five Points."

"Sure. Hard times and good, boyo. So?"

"Be honest. It was mostly hard times."

Bull snorted. "Yeah, so it was."

"Where are we now? All them years of stealing, scraping, running, fighting...where'd it get us? We ain't no better off now than we ever was."

"So? What's your point, boyo?"

"Maybe things don't have to be the way they always were. Maybe we can change, yeah?"

"What? You mean get all gentrified, like Tony wants? Be his dress up dolls, walk and talk and say please and thank you? Not me. No, sir."

"Why?"

"What do you mean?"

Dandy rolled his eyes. "I mean, why not? You know what, boyo? I *like* having nice clothes, and I like the way people look at me when I'm wearing them. I like living in a nice room. Having hot water brought up for a bath whenever I want it, and not having to shit in an outhouse, freezing cold in winter and burning hot in summer. I like eating food that isn't half-rancid, even if it means having to know what fucking fork to use."

Bull's lips tilted in a smirk. "Yeah? Well...me, too. It was nice, huh? While it lasted, I mean."

"Yeah. That's the thing. I don't want to go back to Five Points, Bull. I don't want to go back to the way things used to be, living hand to mouth all the time, stealing to eat and fighting to keep what I stole. I want to stay here, at Club Raven. Maybe not forever, but at least until we can figure out a way to earn money nobody can take away from us."

Bull looked genuinely surprised at the idea. "Huh. I don't know, Dandy. I don't much like taking orders from people. What makes them better than us?"

"They ain't... They're *not* better than us. That's what Tony's been trying to tell us all along. Don't you get it? He's been saying the only difference between us and them swells is the way they dress and talk, and the manners they use. That's what he's been trying to teach us with all the lessons."

"Yeah, that and money, which we don't got." Bull smiled wryly. "I guess I did like how nobody batted an eyelash when we walked into the Great Room. Like we belonged there, or something."

"Exactly, because we *did* belong there." Dandy lifted a shoulder. "Maybe it wouldn't be so bad to stay here, Bull. Take the lessons, become...somebodies."

"Yeah, but you heard Tony. He's throwing us out. We can't go back to him begging."

"No, I suppose not." Dandy slumped, looking crushed, as if the weight of the entire world just settled on his shoulders. Then, he suddenly sat up straight, squaring his shoulders as if shrugging it off. "You know what, boyo? Yes, we can. We can go down there and apologize. Say we're sorry, tell Tony he was right, and that we want to make something of ourselves. Why not? Ain't... *Isn't* nobody stopping us."

Bull sputtered with indignation. "What'll people think if we go crawling back on our bellies like that?"

Dandy sighed. "What'll *who* think? What people are you worried about? The plug-uglies down at the wharfs? The whores at the Soiled Dove? What do we care what anybody thinks of us, even if they was to find out, which they won't. Tony ain't gonna run around telling everybody we said we were wrong. He ain't... *isn't* like that."

"Even so, think he might take us back again? We run off once before, you know, and he was plenty mad then. Imagine he's doubly angry this time."

"I don't know, but we can try, can't we?"

Bull fell silent and seemed to think it over. Then he brightened, smiling. "Okay, boyo. Let's go ask him. What do we have to lose?" He started to get up, but Dandy put out a hand, stopping him.

"Wait a minute, Bull. We may not be in a room as nice as this one, or on a bed as soft and clean, not for a long time, maybe not ever. Tony can wait a few minutes, can't he?" He crawled up on the bed until he reached the headboard, then lay down and pulled Bull into his arms. He reached for a long, deep kiss. "Want to feel my skin against these fancy sheets one more time."

"Want to feel my skin is more like it." Bull chuckled, and sat up. He pulled his shirt up over his head without bothering with the buttons, then went to work on his drawers. "You ain't gonna get undressed? Gonna make me sucking your dick a bit difficult, ain't it?"

Dandy grinned at him, and quickly divested himself of every stitch of clothing except his socks. He flopped back on the mattress, arms and legs spread, cock already hard and bobbing over his stomach.

Bull jumped off the bed and skinnied out of his pants, then hopped up and bounced on the mattress, grinning like a fool. He straddled one of Dandy's legs, trapping it between his knees, and bent over.

Dandy hissed through his teeth when Bull took his cock in, sucking hard and pulling at the delicate flesh with his teeth. Bull's hands didn't remain idle, either; one wrapped around Dandy's length, pulling on the foreskin as he sucked, and the other slid over Dandy's thighs and cupped his balls, giving them an easy yank now and then.

Moaning softly, Dandy arched his back, hips lifting up, pushing his cock deep into Bull's pretty mouth. The wet noises grew louder as Bull seemed to double down on his efforts to suck the come from Dandy's cock.

Then suddenly, Dandy grunted and heaved, flipping the two of them around so that Bull lay on his back and Dandy was looking down at him. Dandy swung his body around until they lay head-to-heel, his cock brushing against Bull's lips as if trying to find its way back into Bull's mouth again, and his own mouth opened to receive Bull's thick length.

Each had his other rhythm as they lavished one another with tongues and lips and teeth, but they also seemed to move in sync, a sweet dance of the oldest variety, but probably still every bit as seductive as it was the very first time a man thought to take another man's dick in his mouth and discovered the pleasure it brought.

Dandy came first, letting go of Bull's cock and throwing his head back, his body stiff in ecstasy. Even as the last shudders ran visibly across his shoulders, he reached for Bull's dick and began stroking it, faster and faster until Bull arched off the bed and came in white spurts across Dandy's face.

Dandy's pink tongue poked out, sweeping across his lips, scooping up Bull's seed, and he smiled. "I do hope Tony lets us stay so we can keep doing this, Bull. I do so enjoy it in a nice, clean bed."

Bull sighed in agreement, then pushed Dandy off him and climbed out of bed, and began searching for the clothes he'd shucked off a few minutes before.

Tony's body shuddered one last time as he worked the last bit of come from his cock. Damn, watching the two of them hadn't grown boring yet. Their bodies were hard and willing, and they made the most amazing sounds when they came. He'd already made up his mind to forgive them and accept them back. It sounded like they'd really learned a lesson, and wanted to improve now. Plus, he would sorely miss watching them fuck.

He was dressed and sitting at the desk in his suite when Walther appeared at his elbow. "Misters Seamus O'Brian and Daniel Gilroy to see you, sir."

Tony looked up from the ledger in which he'd been writing, and cocked his head. That wasn't at all what he'd been expecting. They sounded familiar, but he couldn't place them. "Who? You should know I don't receive visitors in my private suite, Walther. Send them away at once."

Walther remained where he stood. "It's Bull and Dandy, sir. They insisted I introduce them using their proper names."

Oh, that's where he'd heard them before! He smiled, putting down his fountain pen. "Ah, very well. Show them in."

"As you wish, sir."

Walther disappeared briefly, then appeared again at the door to the suite. He opened it and ushered Bull and Dandy inside before disappearing again.

The two of them looked about as comfortable as a king in a hog pen. Their cheeks were splotched with red, and their eyes remained downcast, refusing to meet Tony's gaze. They stood before him, hands balled into fists at their sides.

Apologies did not come easily to these two. Tony smiled, and understood. They hadn't come easy to him, either. Still didn't, truth be told. "Why are you two still here? I thought I told you both to leave."

"About that, Tony..." Dandy began, but looked to Bull for help. He tapped an elbow into Bull's side, making Bull jump.

Bull cast a quick, glowering look at Dandy. "Um, we were wondering if, I mean, we..."

"We're sorry." Dandy blurted out the words as if they tasted rancid on his tongue. "There. I said it."

"Sorry for what?" Tony was beginning to enjoy this, just a little. Maybe more than a little—they'd been like two painful splinters in his ass of late.

Bull gave a small shrug. "Sorry we stole from the members again, and tried to run off."

"Come on, Tony." Dandy risked a glance up. "Don't make us beg."

"Yeah," Bull put in. "It was hard enough giving the money back. Those men looked at us like we was worms, even though we told 'em what you said about it being a college prank."

Tony harrumphed. "You're lucky they believed you and didn't ask me to call in the constable. Your little stunt cost me two cases of our best single malt." He narrowed his eyes at them. "It'll take you a good, long while to pay me back what I've lost."

They looked up at him, again, hope beginning to glow in their eyes, and he had to bite back a smile.

"Then we can stay?" Bull asked.

"Yes, you can stay. If for no other reason than to pay me back for those cases of single malt. That stuff doesn't come cheap." He cocked an eyebrow at them. "The question we have before us now is, in what capacity will you remain here? As students, or as servants?"

"Servants!" Outrage colored Bull's cheeks. "Now, wait just a minute, boyo. We ain't nobody's—"

Dandy elbowed Bull hard enough to draw a squawk. "Shut up, Bull." He looked at Tony, and lifted his chin. "We want to stay, and we want to learn to be real gentlemen. Maybe make a life for ourselves, a real one, where we don't have to steal no more. If that means we got to work as servants, then we'll do it. Won't we, Bull?" He turned and glared at Bull as if to dare Bull to disagree.

Bull's lips pressed together into a thin, white line, as if he was trying to keep the words inside his mouth. When they finally escaped, they sounded breathy. "Fine. Yes. We'll work as servants if you'll keep giving us lessons and such."

Tony sat back, and stroked his chin thoughtfully for a moment or two, giving the impression he was considering their request, then finally nodded. "Good. But I'm warning you two—this is your last chance. If you *ever* give me cause to doubt your honesty within these walls again, I will not simply send you back to Five Points. I will make you sorry you ever popped out of your mamas. Do you understand me?"

"Yes, sir." They spoke in unison, both seeming both relieved and eager. Then Bull frowned.

"Tony? What about Detective Clare? We pummeled him pretty good. He must be in a pucker over it."

"Well, he gave you two more than a bit back, didn't he? Broke Dandy's nose, more than likely, and gave you a black eye."

"Yeah, but he's the law. They don't exactly forgive and forget. And we know Mayor Forge sent him here after us. What if he wants to arrest us?"

"Thomas won't be happy, but no. Detective Clare is now a member of this club, and as such would never insult me by arresting my...apprentices. Besides, after my *talk* with Forge, he isn't interested in you anymore. Anyway, let me worry about Detective Clare. You worry about yourselves."

"Apprentice! I like the sound of that, eh?" Dandy beamed, and Bull looked just as excited. "My pa said I'd never amount to nothing, but look at me, an apprentice!"

"All right. As far as I'm concerned, nothing has changed. You will continue with your lessons. Next month I'll plan a grand soiréefor our special members. It will be your debut party. If you study hard and behave yourselves, then do me proud at the event, I will gift you with a stipend to begin your new lives as gentlemen, be it here in Baltimore, or elsewhere. Are we agreed?"

Their eyes lit up like children who'd just seen candles glowing on a Christmas tree for the first time. Both nodded vigorously.

"Yes, sir! We'll make you proud. Just wait and see." Dandy said, and then turned to look at Bull. They laughed, and then-lunged at each other, hugging and jumping around the room.

"All right, all right! Enough." Tony smirked at them. "Go on back to your room and call the chambermaid to bring up heated water for a bath. You both smell like the upstairs rooms at the Soiled Dove."

Chapter Fifteen

A month later, the club was in an uproar. The servants had been busy for days polishing silverware, washing and drying glasses and dinnerware, ironing linens, peeling and scraping potatoes and vegetables, dusting and polishing everything in the club from the graceful wooden banister on the grand staircase to the tiny crystal teardrops hanging from the immense chandeliers gracing the ballroom. It was a good thing they were ghosts, thus never needing rest or sleep, or Tony would've had to hire on an army of flesh-and-blood workers to do the job, and this party was costing him enough already.

It would be worth it, though to prove to himself and everyone else that everyone, even the lowliest born street rat, could learn to be successful and genteel. He looked at himself in the full length mirror in his suite. He'd had a new dark tail coat and trousers made especially for the evening, and paired them with a green waistcoat embroidered with golden thread, a matching wide, silk ascot tie, and a new top hat. On his feet were highly polished, square-toed shoes. Pristine white gloves completed the outfit.

It was almost a shame he wouldn't be wearing them for long.

He smiled at his reflection and reached for his golden-headed cane. He appeared the very image of a well-dressed gentleman, but the party he had planned would be anything but genteel. His smile widened into a wicked grin. *The members of Club Raven are going to be talking about this party for years to come. Just let Julian and Matthias try to outdo it!*

Walther appeared to his right. "You look quite dapper this evening, sir. Might you be requiring my service this evening?"

"No, Walther. You may join your brethren and enjoy yourself." Traditionally, the ghostly servants would set up the banquet and the ballroom for the party, but then would dissipate like smoke. The dead preferred to watch the goings on of the living from a distance.

Tony left his room. It was early; no one would arrive for another hour at least, but he was anxious to oversee the final details and make certain everything was perfect.

He went directly to the grand ballroom on the second floor. There was an antechamber that was set up as a large changing room for the guests to use before entering the ballroom. Several servants—human, not ghosts—stood quietly in crisply ironed uniforms and starched aprons, ready to aid whichever members needed their aid.

From the antechamber, the guests would move into the ballroom, where a magnificent and unusual feast awaited. This was one dinner his mother would neither cook for nor attend. She had been given orders to remain in her room for the evening. Given an opportunity for a hot soak, knowing others would be cooking and serving in her stead, she would take advantage of her forced leisure and enjoy a night in, Tony knew.

He'd gotten the idea for the party from an old text he'd read about ancient Roman emperors and their fondness—and talent—for throwing the most creative, debauched soirées. Although his party would be a great deal tamer than some of the Roman ones he'd read about, it would still be unparalleled for Baltimore.

Within the ballroom, long tables had been set with spotless white linens upon which a wide selection of delicacies had been artfully arranged. Not on gleaming platters or in crystal bowls as one might expect at such a fashionable event, but on bodies of living men.

He'd enlisted Maude Breem's help in hiring men to work the party, insisting on those with the most beautifully sculpted bodies, handsomest faces, smoothest skin, and sleekest hair that could be found in Baltimore and the surrounding areas. He'd paid exorbitant prices for their participation, but had been rewarded with some of the most exquisite geycats in the area.

Each table held one man, his nude body prone and cleverly draped with grapes, or chocolates, or strawberries, or surrounded by select cuts of cold pheasant and steak tartare, along with crisp stalks of asparagus. At one table, a man lay nearly buried underpyramids built of small, bright oranges, a rare and costly treat at this time of year. Another's smooth skin was drizzled with chocolate, his body surrounded by bowls of clotted cream and plump berries.

Additional geycats, nude except for black ascot ties, stood at the ready in a neat, straight line stretching across the back of the ballroom, each bearing an empty silver tray. When the party began, they would circulate the room offering the members the most delicious and decadent delights of all—themselves.

Unobtrusive, small round tables were conveniently scattered throughout the room bearing oils and various fetishes for the members' use. In one corner, a cross, similar to the one in the playroom, had been erected, complete with shackles and a selection of whips and crops.

Mattresses were laid on the floor along the walls, made over with fine silks and satins, and strewn with fluffy goose feather pillows, awaiting guests who wished more intimate encounters.

Tony walked slowly around the room, inspecting everything, smoothing a minute wrinkle in a table linen on this table, moving a cluster of grapes so that it more perfectly framed a man's nipple on that one. He wanted everything to be perfect. Finally, he nodded and left the ballroom, firmly closing the door behind him.

A pair of menservants dressed in black tail coats and pants, and white vests and gloves, stood sentry on either side of the double doors, ready to pull them open for a grand reveal once all the guests had arrived.

He was expecting a large gathering, perhaps fifty men in total, all of them "special" members of Club Raven. While many men held regular memberships which entitled them to the use of the Great Room and the dining hall, a select number of men, all chosen for the special talents they possessed or connections they could bring the Club Raven owners, were issued *special* membership privileges. It was these few who could gain passage past the watchful eyes of Kwanele, and access to the upper floors of Club Raven, where theycould enjoy the fragrantsteam baths, explore the delights of the playroom, or simply retreat into one of the beautifully appointed guest rooms to indulge their carnal natures.

Club Raven wasn't a bawdy house by any means; it was a place for likeminded men to find one another and feel free to express themselves, exploring their sexuality in a safe and protected space.

And, at times, perhaps, to be enticed and delighted by wickedly outlandish parties, such as the one Tony had planned for this evening.

He pulled his watch from the small pocket on his waistcoat and checked the time. Nearly eight o'clock. The first of his guests would be arriving soon. He hurried through the antechamber, and down to the first floor to greet them as a proper host should.

The anteroom, although large, still had a crowded feel. Men were disrobing, carefully folding and placing their expensive evening wear, shoes, socks, undergarments, and hats in small, neat piles on the provided tables. Most of them knew one another, having attended events at Club Raven on prior occasions, and chatted and laughed as they readied themselves. A few, caught up in the excitement, were already groping one another or sharing open-mouthed kisses.

Servants began circulating the room with trays bearing glasses of champagne. By the time Tony reached the room, having waited downstairs to greet the last on the guest list to arrive, everyone held a glass. Once he'd divested himself of his clothing, he also took up a glass and called for the crowd's attention.

"My dear friends, welcome! We at Club Raven have once again arranged for a party to entertain and delight our special members. While any reason is good reason for us to come together to celebrate, tonight is very special for me. I would like to take this opportunity to introduce to you two young men whom I have taken a special interest in. Kindly join me in welcoming to the Club Raven family Master Seamus O'Brian, heir to the O'Brian Shipping dynasty, and Master Daniel Gilroy, whose family owns Gilroy Mercantile, of Dublin, London, and Manhattan, my new apprentices."

Polite applause filled the room and necks craned to see the men lucky enough to have been taken under Tony Brazzio's wing. As co-owner of Club Raven, he had access to every luxury known to the modern world, and the means to satisfy every desire. Tony could tell from the avarice glittering in so many of the members' eyes that there probably wasn't a single man in the room who didn't envy the apprentices their positions.

He bit back a smile and raised his glass toward the door to the anteroom. It was the cue the servant at the door had been waiting for. The door opened, and Bull and Dandy walked in.

Or rather, he reminded himself, *Seamus and Daniel.* Much like their old lives as petty thieves and scoundrels, they were giving up their coarse nicknames in favor of their given names. Tony had made up from whole cloth the bits about Seamus being the son of shipping magnate, and Daniel being heir to a mercantile empire, but he knew no one in the room would question it. The men here all had little fabrications they liked to hide behind. Not because their true identities were kept secret—a member would rather die than reveal his brethren's names to anyone not a part of Club Raven's inner circle; it was an oath they took upon receiving membership, and one they took very seriously—but because of the element of excitement such stories could bring to an encounter. One never knew who a man might claim to be from one night to the next. Sometimes men claimed they were Arabian sheiks, or Indian chiefs, or Greek gods come back to earth. There were men who liked to dress in women's clothing, wearing satins and lace, and powdering their faces, while other men like to wear Stetson hats and chaps although they'd never been further west than the Allegheny Mountains. Whatever the fantasy, it all added spice to what might perhaps be an otherwise ordinary evening.

Just as Tony had hoped, the guests accepted Seamus and Daniel as exactly who he claimed them to be, and fifty glasses lifted and clinked in a welcoming toast.

Tony smiled warmly at Seamus and Daniel, hugging each one in turn. He'd prepared them earlier, explaining they'd be walking into a room full of naked men, and they did well, showing no surprise. After hugging Tony and draining their glasses, they moved off and began to undress. He would be sure to watch them throughout the evening to see how they interacted with the members and otherwise deported themselves, but so far they seemed to be doing a fine job, indeed.

Thomas Clare was there as well, seemingly glued at the hip to Leopold. Tony smiled as he watched Leopold wrap a black leather collar around Thomas's neck. It was attached to a long, golden chain, and once it was in place, Thomas squatted down and looked up at Leopold with the eager, loving expression of a faithful puppy. Leopold held the chain, and gave it a little yank now and then, as if to remind Thomas who the Master was, although Tony didn't think Thomas needed any reminding.

Those two make a good pair, he thought, and felt a little proud at being the one who brought them together. He knew Leopold serviced other men as well, but there seemed to be something special growing between Leopold and Thomas.

He lifted his glass, clinking the ruby ring he'd slipped on his pinkie for the occasion against the crystal, and waited for the crowd to settle and turn toward him. "My dear guests, dinner awaits!" He nodded toward the menservants guarding the doors to the ballroom, their cue to push the doors open and allow access to the members.

Tony waited patiently outside as his fifty guests filed into the ballroom, but he could hear their delighted gasps and excited murmuring. From the sound of things, his party was going to be a great success, and he was grinning broadly as he handed his glass to a servant and followed the last of them inside.

Chapter Sixteen

Within the hour, the party was in full swing.

The geycats in their ascots walked the room, a silver platter supporting their balls. Most had erections, obviously enjoying the uniqueness of the night as much as the patrons. Tony watched as one of the members, a man named Lester Briggs, signaled one of the geycats to his knees. The geycat obeyed instantly, opening his mouth to receive Briggs's dick.

On two of the buffet tables, the one with the oranges—which had been swiftly toppled, rolling every which way across the ballroom floor—and the one with the berries, men were enthusiastically fucking.

On one, Russell Eddington had his cock shoved inside the ass of Patrick Rheingold, who in turn was fucking the luscious rear end of the geycat who'd been so recently on display along with the oranges. The three of them rocked and grunted in unison, and had attracted a small gather of watchers, all with dicks in hand.

The other table held Victor Meyer, owner of some of the largest sawmills in the northeast. He lay on his back, his cock being ridden by an energetic young man, whose body was smeared with clotted cream and streaks of berry juice.

Tony fisted his cock with slow, leisurely backstrokes as he walked the room. He didn't want to come yet—he was having too good a time watching the others fuck and suck their way into orgasms. Many had already sated themselves; the air was heavy with the smell of sex. Those who had were off in one corner sipping brandies and smoking cigars, their wilted dicks hanging heavy between their thighs. Some of them were virile enough to come back for a second go-round shortly, but others would be find their way into the anteroom, dress, and slip away into the night before long.

He drifted over toward an area of the room where a pedestal had been erected. On it, a handsome, blond young man with skin like alabaster stood. A half dozen men gathered around him, dipping their fingers into bowls of melted chocolate, and thenusing them to paint lovely designs on his flesh. No sooner had a swirl been added to the young man's skin, than a tongue slid along after it, lapping up the sweet treat. Tony watched as one man fisted a chocolate-covered hand over the geycat's cock, coating it in rich chocolate, then taking the length in fully. By the time the man had licked and sucked the chocolate off, the geycat was moaning, his eyes dark and hooded, and his full lips parted.

Not far from the artist's corner, Tony spotted Seamus and Daniel. They were kneeling on a mattress, their legs spread, jerking off as a pair of men knelt behind them, fingering their holes. He noticed their backs were streaked with drying come—they'd been both busy and popular tonight, a good sign that the members had accepted them.

Two strong arms suddenly encircled his waist, and a thick cock pressed against his backside, hard and hot. "You have a lovely cock, sir. May I help you with that?"

He smiled and turned his head. The geycat was strikingly handsome, having dark, swarthy skin and the brightest blue eyes Tony had seen in a good, long while. With a firm body, sculpted and shaved of all body hair, the young man was exquisite. "Have you a name?"

"Michael."

"Like the archangel?" He grinned when Michael ground his cock against his ass and chuckled.

"Well, I'm told I have a fiery sword."

"Indeed." Tony turned around to face Michael, and pulled him in for a deep, wet kiss. His hands slid over the smooth skin of Michael's back, delighting in the play of muscles under them, until they reached plump, twin globes. "Lovely ass. Delightful." He gave them a squeeze, and pulled Michael's hips closer, letting their cocks press together.

"It's yours if you want it. Or I'll fuck you...whatever you wish. I'm eager to please." Michael gave Tony's ass an answering squeeze.

He smirked. "How very generous of you. Still, I have a better idea." He led Michael to a table and, with one stroke of his arm, swept an array of silver plates and cutlery to the floor. He patted the now-empty tabletop. "Hop up here, won't you?"

Michael grinned at him and did as he asked, sitting on the edge of the table, his thick erection listing to one side. "Want to suck me?"

"Now, now. It's my choice, I believe. On your hands and knees."

Michael's eyes widened for only the briefest of moments, but he did as Tony ordered.

Tony nudged Michael's thighs apart, giving himself a better view of Michael's heavy balls. They were hairless as well, he noticed. *Brave man, letting someone near his jewels with a straight razor.* He grabbed a few supplies from one of the tables and returned, laying his provisions out within easy reach.

He began with one of his favorite oils, imported and scented heavily with sandalwood. He drizzled it between Michael's ass cheeks, using his fingers to work it into the crack and over Michael's hole.

Once Michael was lubricated, Tony slipped a finger into the tight hole. He hissed through his teeth as hot, silken walls clenched at his finger and squeezed. His cock bobbed as if jealous of his hand and he rewarded it with a few slow strokes.

"So fucking tight. Such a delightful hole." He slipped his finger in and out, twisting it and turning it as he did until Michael began to react. "Like that? I think you do." He pushed a second finger in next to the first.

He noticed a few men gathering behind him, watching. Good. An exhibitionist as well as a voyeur, he liked to be watched almost as much as he liked watching.

Three fingers were now buried in Michael's asshole, fucking him noisily with the help of additional oil. Tony was quite liberal with it—Michael's balls were shiny with oil and it puddled on the tabletop between his knees. The smell of sandalwood competed with the smell of semen, combining into a heady fragrance that stirred Tony's blood and stiffened his cock further.

"Can you take another finger?" Tony asked as he kissed and nibbled at the delicate flesh of Michael's ass.

Michael's answer was breathy. "I can take whatever you want to give me."

Tony smiled, and slowly added a fourth, well-oiled finger beside the initial three. Murmuring behind him told him the men who'd gathered to watch now knew what was coming, and approved. They groaned, and he could hear the wet sound of cocks being jerked.

Finally, Tony removed his fingers and doused them once again with oil. Michael's asshole was already gaping; that Tony would fuck it was given. For now, he wanted Michael to feel the burn, the stretch, to feel his hand inside Michael's ass. Pressing his fingertips together he slowly inched all five fingers into Michael's hole.

They slid in, Michael's body stretching to accommodate them, and Tony moaned as Michael's body molded itself around his hand. He didn't move it, didn't try to fuck Michael with his hand. He just stood still, letting them both enjoy the sensations.

"God, you're tight! Yes, squeeze that beautiful ass around my hand. Fuck!"

Michael's head hung down, and he was panting. "Please, fuck me! I want to come. Let me come!"

"As you wish," Tony answered, and pulled his hand out of Michael's ass. He used the tablecloth to wipe it clean.

Tony pulled Michael off the table, catching him when his knees wobbled. "Lean over the table."

When Michael did as he ordered, he positioned himself and slid into Michael's body in one effortless motion. Fully seated up to his balls, he gripped Michael's hips, fingers digging in. "Fuck!"

His climax was biting at the bit, and he knew he wouldn't be able to keep it at bay much longer. He began to thrust, riding Michael's plump ass, flesh slapping flesh, until his desire built to a crescendo, to a point so sharp it could draw blood, then broke free from his control. He threw his head back and howled his pleasure toward the ceiling, spilling his seed deep inside Michael's body.

Michael shuddered underneath him, his hand working his cock as he came shortly after, then lay against the table, breathing hard. His body trembled even as Tony's cock slid free from it.

A smattering of applause reminded Tony he'd had an audience, a satisfied one by the sound of things.

Michael twisted his head, looking at Tony from over his shoulder. His eyes were hooded and a bit unfocussed. "That was amazing."

"Never had a man's hand up your ass before?" Tony helped Michael up, although he didn't urge Michael to sit down. It would be awhile before that particular action would be comfortable.

Michael shook his head. "This was my first time. I'd heard of it, but never..." His smile was a little shaky. "I think my ass will remember you for quite some time."

Tony leaned down and kissed him. "You did well. I'll ask Maude for you again soon." He cupped Michael's cheek, and gave it a little squeeze and patted it, then turned away.

The crowd of fifty had thinned considerably. Only a few men remained, small pockets of them gathered here and there around the ballroom. He padded out into the anteroom, and swiftly dressed. A check of his pocket watch revealed the time was nearing midnight. He grinned to himself. *How time does fly when one has one's hand up another man's ass!* It was time to call an end to the festivities.

He returned to the ballroom, and raised his voice to be heard. "I fear all good things come to an end, and the hour grows late, gentlemen. Servants wait in the anteroom to help you dress. Your carriage drivers have been notified that you'll be departing soon." He smiled and nodded as men passed and offered him thanks for a most enjoyable evening.

He followed the last of them out of the ballroom, closing the door behind him. The geycats would exit using the servants' staircase at the rear of the ballroom. Their clothes were waiting in one of the empty rooms on the first floor, along with packets containing their fees.

Seamus and Daniel were among the last men to leave the ballroom, and they stopped to thank Tony.

"Sure, and we made the right decision, boyo. That was some party you threw for us!" Seamus's face was flushed, but his smile was genuine.

"That it was, indeed!" Daniel nodded. "Me cock emptied three times. If I went one more go-round, I think it might fall right off my body!" He yawned so loudly his jaw cracked.

Tony laughed, and patted the two of them on the backs. "Best get dressed and get upstairs to bed, boys. It's been a long night for everyone. We'll talk about your plans for the future tomorrow."

Seamus blinked at him. "The future?"

"Of course," Tony said. "Have you forgotten? Part of our agreement was that I'd give you both a stipend to start new lives."

Daniel shook his head, and opened his mouth as if to demur, but a sharp elbow in the ribs from Seamus clamped his lips shut again.

"Don't you be telling Tony what he can and can't do, now. If he wants to set up us, who are we to tell him no?" Seamus said. He turned to Tony. "We'll see you in the morning."

Tony grinned and watched them walk away, arm in arm. There was real affection between the two of them. He'd make sure they were well settled, wherever they chose to go after leaving Club Raven.

There was always some confusion after a party, as men scouted for missing gloves, misplaced hats, and tried to find the mates of mismatched shoes, and Tony was soon caught up in it. Men hopped on one foot trying to pull on boots, bumping into others who were trying to button their flies. Still others had drunk far too much and swayed and hung heavily on the shoulders of whoever they could grab, throwing others off balance.

It was a madhouse, but the Club Raven servants had been through it many times, and were well prepared to handle it. With an ease that impressed Tony every time, they sorted out garments and helped dress men who were having a difficult time of it.

It was just as the last of them were dressed and being escorted down to the first floor, that the screams began.

Chapter Seventeen

Tony took the stairs two and three at a time, almost vaulting down from landing to landing. A small crowd of men stood at the doors to the Great Room. Above their heads was Kwanele's face, stoic and unforgiving. No doubt the huge warrior was blocking their access to the room.

He pushed past the men, and sidled past Kwanele. "Close the doors and keep anyone from entering," he said. Kwanele nodded to him and did as he was ordered, to the obvious dismay of the lookers on. No one would dare try to force themselves past Kwanele, though, and Tony knew it. Unless Tony bade them entry, nobody would be setting foot in the Great Room.

Near the fireplace, he saw Thomas kneeling next to a prone figure. He walked closer and noticed blood splattered on the marble hearth and pooling darkly on the floor. Shock stole the breath from his lungs when he looked down at the face of the man lying dead on the floor.

It was Leopold. Someone had slit his throat.

The front of his formerly white shirt was crimson, soaked through with his blood, and his expression was anything but peaceful. Although his eyes were already taking on the milky cauls of death, they were wide open, and the expression frozen in them seemed one of terror.

"Who could have done such a thing?" Thomas looked up at Tony, his expression etched with deep lines of regret. "He was so special. He...knew me, knew what I needed. Why would someone want to kill him?"

"I don't know, Thomas."

Thomas stood up and seemed to straighten his spine. "Don't touch anything, please. Send someone for the police, Tony. And I'll need a list of the names of every man who attended the party."

Tony's eyes popped wide. "I can't do that, Thomas. You know that. Our members' privacy is of the utmost importance."

Thomas squared off with Tony, glaring at him. "No, finding the person responsible for killing Leopold is what's important here!"

Tony placed a hand on Thomas's arm, but he shrugged it off. "Listen to me, Thomas. I know you were fond of Leopold, but..."

"But what? He was a geycat, so he was dispensable? His death is less important? Meaningless?"

"No, of course not! That's not what I meant. There must be some way for us to investigate without sacrificing our members' anonymity." Tony scowled, an idea dancing just out of reach. Then it came to him. "Of course! Walther!" He called out, and was rewarded when Walther immediately appeared at his side.

"Sir?"

"Did you or any of the other servants see what happened here?"

"I'm afraid not, sir. We were otherwise indisposed."

Thomas glowered at Walther. "What do you mean? Where were you and the others?"

"We were released from our duties," Walther replied, as if that explained everything. To Tony, it did, but he knew the staff far better than Thomas did.

"He means they were incorporeal," Tony said. "Our servants are ghosts, Thomas—something, I might add, the local constabulary would not understand or believe. When they aren't working, they...dissipate. It's difficult to explain, but they cease to have physical forms. None of them could have done this. Nor would they, even if they could. Our servants are completely faithful to Club Raven and its patrons."

Thomas turned away, his hands tucked behind his back. "Someone must have seen something!"

An idea occurred to Tony then, and he almost smiled. "Walther, fetch Seamus and Daniel here at once."

Walther blinked lazily. "Who, sir?"

Tony rolled his eyes in frustration. "Oh, for heaven's sake... Bull and Dandy."

"Ah, the thieves. At once, sir." He faded away.

"Why call for them? What can they do?" Thomas asked.

Tony couldn't help the small smile lifting his lips. "For one thing, I think they can tell us who murdered Leopold."

When Seamus and Daniel entered the room, they both looked disheveled and bleary-eyed. Their hair was wild, and their shirts were untucked and miss buttoned. Both had quite a bit to drink at the party, and combined with the healthy bouts of sex they'd enjoyed, they'd practically fallen asleep before their bodies came in contact with their mattress. Daniel was sure Walther must've had a job waking them up and getting them decent enough to appear in the public areas of the club.

"What's going on, Tony? We were sleeping, boyo. Been a hard night, yeah?" Seamus was rubbing his eyes with his fists.

Daniel came in on his heels. "Walther wouldn't tell us why you wanted us to come down here..." Daniel's voice trailed off as his gaze flicked from Tony to Thomas to the body lying on the floor. "Oh, my God! Who is that? What's happened?"

"Mother of God, that's Leopold!" Seamus gasped, and clapped a hand over his mouth. "Sweet Jaysus, what happened?"

"We're hoping you can tell us." Tony put a gentle hand on Daniel's arm. "Here's your chance to do something good for the benefit of the club, Dandy. I need you to use your power to see if you can tell us who did this awful thing."

"Oh, no, no, I couldn't possibly do it." Daniel shook his head, and took several steps backward. He felt the blood drain from his face, leaving him feeling a bit woozy and lightheaded. "I would have to touch him. I ain't never touched a dead body before. Not even at me grandmother's funeral."

"Please Dandy." Tony put his hand on the small of Daniel's back, urging him forward. "If you don't, we'll have to call in the police, and that will cause enormous problems for the club."

Daniel looked into Tony's eyes, his own expression reflecting his terror. Still, he knew how much he owed the club and Tony. And there was that stipend he and Bull...er, Seamus were going to receive. He certainly didn't want to jeopardize their chances at a better future, but the thought of touching a corpse, of getting near all that blood, made him feel sick to his stomach. "Can't you give me something of his instead?"

Tony frowned. "What do you mean?"

"Well, if I hold something he was wearing or holding when he was killed, I might be able to see who did it." Daniel glanced at the body, then quickly looked away. "What's that chain in his hand?"

Thomas sighed. "Leopold had me wear a collar tonight." His voice cracked when he spoke Leopold's name. "That chain was attached to it." He bent and gently untangled the chain from Leopold's fingers. When he stood up, he stared for a few long minutes at the golden chain he held, spotted with Leopold's blood, but then turned and walked over to where Daniel stood near the door. He held it out for Daniel to take.

Daniel eyes the blood splattered chain, loath to touch it. "Isn't there anything else? Something not covered in gore?"

Seamus poked Daniel with an elbow. "Have pity, boyo. Be a man and take the damnable thing."

Daniel scowled at Seamus. Still, the sooner he got this over with, the sooner he could leave the room and the corpse behind him. He swallowed hard, then reached for the chain.

He was completely unprepared for the images and emotions that came so fast and hard they practically knocked him off his feet. His knees wobbled and gave out, and he was only dimly aware of Seamus catching him and lowering him to the ground.

He was in the Great Room, but he wasn't himself. He was looking at the world through Leopold's eyes. "Thomas is taking longer than I expected to get dressed, but he wants to see me home. Such a sweet man. I've come into the Great Room to wait for him." Daniel's fingers slid over the chain as he talked, although he didn't feel it. Flecks of blood stained his fingers. "I'm standing in front of the fire, warming myself.

"I hear the door open, and I think it's Thomas, but when I turn to look..." Daniel gasped, his eyes flying open wide. "What are you doing here?"

"Who is it, Dandy?" Tony knelt down next to Daniel and Seamus. "Who's there?"

"You're not invited to this party. It's a private affair." Daniel made shooing motions with his hands, softly rattling the chain. "Go on and leave. I've nothing to say to you." Daniel didn't hear the cries of the other men in the room demanding he tell them what he was seeing. His body was in the present with them, but his mind was caught in the past, seeing and hearing only what Leopold had. "What right do you have to come in here? What are you doing? Get away from me! Get away!"

Pain, diamond bright, slashed across his throat, releasing a fountain of crimson. He pressed his hands to his throat as if to stem the flow. "Why? Why?"

More quickly than he would've imagined, darkness began to

creep into the edges of his vision. His body grew cold, so cold, and his legs gave out. He fell to the floor, and as the blackness finally took him, his last thoughts were of Thomas.

A shudder wracked Daniel's body, and the chain clattered to the floor. He gasped, tears stinging his eyes, and fell against Seamus. He never, ever wanted to go through anything like that again. This was not using his gift to find out where a man kept his billfold, or where Bull lost the key to his mother's flat. This was the most godawful experience of Daniel's life, and one he never wanted repeated.

Seamus's arms wrapped around him, pulling him close. "What did you see, boyo? Did you see who killed him?"

"Yes. Oh, Sweet Jaysus, it was as if I was him. I felt it, Bull. Felt him dying." He shuddered again, and buried his face in Seamus's shirt.

Tony petted Daniel's hair, soothing him. "Who was it, Daniel? It sounded like Leopold knew whoever attacked him."

Daniel kept his face pressed to Seamus's chest, but he nodded. "He did. So do you. So do we all."

Thomas's voice was tight and his obvious anger barely controlled. "Who *was* it?"

Daniel's answer was more of a sob than a sentence. "It was Gideon Forge."

Tony gaped at him. "The *mayor?*" Why would Gideon Forge want to kill Leopold?"

Thomas's face went milk white. He turned his back on them, looking again at Leopold's body. "To get at us. Oh, God, this is our fault. It's our doing he's dead!"

"What are you talking about, Thomas?" Tony spun Thomas around, his hands on Thomas's shoulders. "What do you mean it's our fault?"

"When we went to his office, what did you tell him, Tony?" Thomas's expression was stricken, and his eyes and nose were running.

Tony looked confused. "I...I suggested that he didn't want to chase Bull and Dandy anymore. I told him they hadn't stolen his pocket watch after all, that he'd misplaced it, they found it and returned it to him."

Thomas nodded. "When you opened the door to leave, I heard you mention planning a party at Club Raven."

"That's true," Tony said. "I did, but what of it?"

"Don't you see? Your power made Forge forget about Bull and Dandy, yes, but he remembered that I still knew his secret! I knew about his forays to the Soiled Dove, and what he did there." Thomas thrust his fingers into his hair, twisting them in the strands. "Oh, God! He must've had me followed, but I'd been so caught up in my relationship with Leopold that I never noticed! He came here tonight to kill me to keep his secret safe, but when he found Leopold, he couldn't resist. He killed Leopold to hurt me, because he's an evil, sadistic bastard."

"Oh, God. I...I'm so sorry, Thomas." Tony looked almost as pale as Thomas. "I never thought he would come after you. How stupid I was to think he was only concerned with Seamus and Daniel."

Thomas's jaw tightened, and he spoke through grit teeth. "I'm going to find him, and I'm going to kill him." He began to move past Tony toward the door.

Tony shook his head and grabbed Thomas's elbow. "Hold up. You're not going alone. I'll go with you."

Thomas threw off his hand. "I don't need your help!"

"Yes, you do. Don't make me use my power to keep you from going off half-cocked, not until you've heard me out. I will if I need to, Thomas." Tony glared at him.

Thomas paused, scowling. "I'm a seasoned police officer. I can find Forge on my own."

"I know, but it'll be quicker with my help. Besides, I've got a stake in this, too. The reputation and honor of Club Raven is at stake here. My mistake brought this tragedy into our house. I need to help right it." Tony stood tall, staring down Thomas.

Daniel wasn't sure Tony would win in the end, but Thomas finally conceded. "Fine. Come along, but remember, when it comes time to kill him, Forge is mine."

"We'll cross that bridge when we come to it." Tony looked down at Seamus and Daniel. "Daniel, thank you so much for what you did here tonight. I know it was brutally difficult for you."

Daniel nodded. "Can we go now, Tony? I can't stand being in here any longer."

"Of course. Go on up to your room." Tony held out a hand, first helping Daniel up, then Seamus. "Get some rest."

As they left, they heard Tony order Walther to gather a few supplies for him,then take Leopold's body to the garden, and to clean up the Great Room. Walther left but returned quickly with a burlap sack, which he handed to Tony.

With a promise that they'd see to Leopold's funeral arrangements in the morning, Tony and Thomas left.

For now, Daniel thought sadly, they had more important things to do—like catch a murderer.

Chapter Eighteen

Gideon Forge lived with his wife in a stately brick manor not far from City Hall. While not as ostentatious as some of the mansions men of more ample means built, his two-story house was an obvious bid at respectability. Tony supposed the house had once possessed an understated, genteel, cultured façade, but the fancy gardens, scrolled ironwork, and stained glass windows were artifice, added to make certain anyone who saw the house immediately knew it was the abode of a powerful and wealthy man.

Tony understood much more about Gideon Forge by looking at this home than he had actually after meeting the man. Forge was one of those men who needed respect the way drunkards needed liquor. Indeed, he didn't care how he got it, as long as he did. In short, Forge wanted what Tony had—power, money, and the esteem of the wealthiest men in Baltimore.

If Forge thought connections with Baltimore's elite would come with his election as mayor, he must've been sorely disappointed. Governor, perhaps. Senator or congressman, certainly, but mayor? The office of mayor was too far down the social ladder to attract the attention of the powerful men who claimed membership at Club Raven.

"The lamps are burning on the first floor. He must be in there." Thomas pointed to a window at the far corner of the building.

Tony nodded. "I see it." He grabbed Thomas's arm when Thomas withdrew his revolver. "You're not going to shoot him,

Thomas. I can't allow that."

"I'm not going to kill him. Not yet. I want to hear him confess first."

"Listen to me. His wife is at home—he may not be, and either way, we can't afford any witnesses. Let me do this. If he's there I can bring him out, and wipe her memory clean if she's present."

Thomas's voice oozed with sarcasm. "Because using your power worked so well for us before?"

"That's not fair, Thomas. We're both to blame for this."

"I know. I'm sorry. Okay, let's go."

They trotted up the walk to the door, and rapped the knocker several times. After a long while, the door cracked open and a servant girl wearing a wrapper answered. "The Mister and Missus is sleeping. Go away, now."

Thomas stuck his foot in the door when the servant attempted to close it. "I think not. I am Detective Thomas Arthur Clare, and I demand to see Mayor Forge."

The girl's eyes grew wide. "But the Mister said I ain't to let nobody in."

"So, he's home? Excellent." Thomas pushed in past the girl, and Tony followed behind him.

Tony placed a gentle hand on the girl's shoulder. "We're not here. This is a dream. Go back to bed. In the morning, you'll know it was just a dream."

"Just a dream. I'm awful tired." The girl yawned, and then padded off down a hallway. A moment later, Tony heard a door open and close.

To their left was a parlor, and beyond it a short hallway. There was a door at the end of the hallway with light showing beneath it. Thomas gestured toward it.

When they got to the door, Thomas raised his revolver and put his hand on the doorknob. With one swift movement, he shoved the door open and stepped inside. Tony crowded in behind him, and closed the door.

Gideon Forge was sitting at his desk in his shirtsleeves, a bottle of amber liquid and a half empty glass before him. His eyes widened and his jaw popped open when he saw them. "What is the meaning of this? Clare? What are you doing? This is my home!" His eyes were bloodshot and, from his slurred speech, he was well on his way to getting drunk.

Tony could see dark streaks striping his white shirt. He didn't have to examine them any closer to know what those splashes were. "Where were you tonight, Gideon?"

"Aren't you that Italian man who came to my office the other day? What are you doing here? I insist the two of you leave immediately!" Forge picked up the bottle and splashed amber liquid into his glass. "A man can't enjoy a nightcap in his own home."

Tony stepped around Thomas and leaned over Forge's desk, planting his hands firmly. He made eye contact with Forge, and pinned him in place with a push of his power. "Answer me. Where were you tonight?"

"I...I was at Club Raven." Forge looked aghast that he'd spoken the words, as if his mouth was a traitor to his brain. He clamped a hand over it, as if to silence it.

"That's all I need to know," Thomas said. He leveled his gun at Forge.

"Stop it, Thomas. Put that away." Tony sent out a push of his talent, this time in Thomas's direction. He had to keep the situation from spiraling out of control. If Thomas shot Forge, someone was sure to hear it—another of the servants, Forge's wife, a neighbor. There was no way to know who might hear, or what witnesses they may leave behind. It was far too risky.

Besides, Tony didn't want another death, no matter how despicable the man was, on his conscience.

Thomas's hand shook as it returned the gun to its holster, but he did as Tony demanded.

Tony turned his attention back to Forge. "Get up, your Honor. We're going for a walk."

"A walk? At this hour? We'll catch our deaths!"

Tony was beginning to get a headache. That happened if he used his power too much within a short period of time, but it couldn't be helped. He pushed again. "Get. Up."

"I...I think a stroll would be most agreeable." Forge hefted his bulk from the chair, and walked around the desk, his steps unsteady.

The stopped only to allow him to get his overcoat, and only then because anyone who might see them would think it odd that a man would be out walking in his shirtsleeves on a such a crisp, cold night. The last thing Tony knew they needed was to be memorable to anyone who might spot them.

Happily, no one else in the house seemed to take notice of their leaving. Forge's wife must've been upstairs in their bedroom, and the servants had all turned in for the night. They left the house without being seen.

He and Thomas had previously decided where to take Forge once they found him. It was necessary—it was too much of a risk to spend so much time inside Forge's home. There was small warehouse located at the wharfs, one that supplied Club Raven with fresh fish caught daily in Chesapeake Bay. It would be empty at this hour, and was secluded enough to afford them privacy.

The march to the wharfs was long and cold. It was over a mile from Forge's house to the wharfs, fighting the chill wind every step of the way. They kept out of the reach of lamplight, three dark blotches against the blacker shadows, moving relentlessly toward the bay. Every so often Forge would begin to complain, either about the cold or his sore feet, and Tony needed to use his power again to keep Forge moving. By the time they finally reached the warehouse, his head was pounding.

Thomas broke out a small pane of glass on the door and, sticking his arm through it, twisted open the lock. The door swung open, and the three of them stumbled inside. It wasn't much warmer inside the building than out, but it was good to be out of the wind, at least.

The smell of fish permeated the building, but their noses swiftly grew tolerant of the stench. They marched Forge past rows of empty crates, all of which would be filled with fresh fish by midmorning, to an office at the rear of the building.

Inside the room, they sat Forge in a chair. Tony pulled candles out of his sack, and lit them. The flames cast dancing shadows across their faces. "All right, Mayor Forge. You said you went to Club Raven tonight. Why?"

Forge's face reddened. "You said you were planning a party. I heard from...erm, a mutual acquaintance when it was to be held, and what sort of party it was going to be." His eyes narrowed at Tony. "Why am I not invited to join Club Raven? I'm the mayor. I'm an important man in this town!"

Tony gave a push. "That's not important. First, tell me who this mutual acquaintance is."

The color on Forge's cheeks deepened from red to scarlet. "A whore they call 'Peanut' at the Soiled Dove."

That explained it. Peanut was probably one of the geycats they'd hired from Maude Breem. "Very good. Now tell me why you went to Club Raven tonight."

"I...wanted to see what the fuss was all about. What was so special about it."

"Don't lie to me." Tony pushed again.

"Fine! I wanted to find him," Forge said. He pointed to Thomas. "He knows about me, about my secrets. I had him followed for a few days, and found out about his lover, and that he was spending time at Club Raven. It wasn't fair. He's nothing but a detective, a nobody, but he can have a lover and go to the swankiest club in the city?" Forge bared his teeth at Thomas. "I hated him for it, hated that he knew my secrets, and had the life I wanted, but I couldn't very well call him into my office and shoot him down right there on my Persian rug, now could I? I didn't trust any of my men to do it, either, not and keep quiet about it. I thought if I caught him here, alone, I'd be able to do away with him, and no one would be the wiser." He smirked. "I figured the owners of Club Raven wouldn't want police or reporters involved if they found a dead body in their club, and would take care of the mess for me."

"You bastard! You killed Leopold!" Thomas's face was a mottled purple, his eyes filled with murderous fury.

"Yes, I killed him. Slit his fucking throat." Forge had the audacity to look proud of his accomplishment, and Tony almost let Thomas shoot him dead on the spot. "I recognized him in an instant. Oh, he was surprised to see me, all right. Didn't expect it, not from me. Stupid, fucking ten-cent whore."

Tony pressed on. "Why would you kill him? What did he ever do to you?"

Forge laughed. "Do? He did *nothing* to me, and that's the problem. He refused me as a client, me, the mayor." He pointed at Thomas. "Refused me, but took this bastard on? A nothing, a no account, ill-bred, ignorant asshole? Why? Why wasn't I good enough? Not good enough for Club Raven, not even good enough for a cheap whore to whip. I couldn't let him live, not when I had the opportunity to make him pay."

Thomas reached for his gun again, but Tony sent out a push to both men. "Listen to me very carefully, Forge. You are going to resign your post as mayor, effective immediately. You are going to pack up your house, your wife, and your servants and move out of Baltimore. If you don't follow my orders to the let-ter, I will let Detective Thomas shoot you down like the dog you are. Do you understand?"

It took another push to get the mayor to agree. By the time they were one, Tony felt like his brains were going to leak out of his ears. He couldn't think of a time in his life, not even back in Five Points, when he'd used his power as often or as forcefully as he had tonight.

"That's it? We just let him walk away?" Thomas was fuming, his face still red and his muscles bunched. A tic made his eyebrow jump. Tony hadn't seen anyone as angry in a long while.

"Yes, that's it. Not for his sake, but for ours, Thomas. For you, for me, for Club Raven, it's best to let it go. Leopold wouldn't have wanted you to destroy yourself or your career by shooting the mayor."

"But he's a murderer! I'm sworn to arrest bastards like this."

"I know, I know. Look, let's just go back to Club Raven. Let Forge find his own way home." Tony's lips curved in a tiny smile as he dug into the burlap sack he'd been carrying. He pulled out a bottle of whiskey and a glass, and set both on the table next to where Forge sat. "Have a good night, Mayor. Remember what you've promised."

They left feeling Forge's glare burning holes in their back. From the corner of his eye, Tony caught sight of Forge reaching for the bottle of liquor.

Chapter Nineteen

Several days later, Tony awoke late the in morning and went down to have breakfast in the kitchen. He found Thomas already awake, along with Seamus and Daniel. Mama was serving them breakfast.

Walther appeared, carrying the newspaper, and handed it to Tony.

It was an extra edition put out by the *Baltimore Gazette*. The headline screamed, *Mayor Found Drowned at Wharfs!* Tony unfolded the paper and read the article aloud. "Mayor Gideon Forge, missing since Saturday night last, was found this dead this morning by fishermen, floating in the water off the wharfs. Police speculate he drowned whenhe fell off the wharf into the freezing water of Chesapeake Bay. While it is unknown what business brought the mayor to the wharfs, foul play is not suspected due to a well-documented fondness for strong drink."

"Well, the bastard got just what he deserved, is what I say." Seamus speared a sausage from a plate Mama put on the table.

"Yeah, good riddance to bad rubbish," Daniel added. "I only hope he suffered after what he did to poor Leopold."

Tony exchanged a knowing glance with Thomas, then let his gaze dart toward Mama. They couldn't afford to say too much in front of her—he didn't want her privy to official club business, particularly when it involved dead bodies. "I can't say I'm not surprised he's gone. He was a drunkard. I guess it was only a matter of time before his drinking killed him."

"Well, thank you for breakfast, ma'am." Thomas drank the

last of the coffee in his mug. "I'll be needed at City Hall this morning, I should think. They'll have to hold a special election, I suppose."

"Will you run? Put yourself on the ballot, and I'll vote for you." Tony smiled at him. "I think many others would, too."

"Me? Mayor? Oh, no. I wouldn't know the first thing about how to run a city." Thomas shook his head, and tried to laugh it off.

Tony could tell Thomas thought the idea far too interesting to easily discard, though. Tony knew Thomas would mull it over, chew on it, and in the end he wasn't convinced Thomas Arthur Clare's name wouldn't be listed on the ballot at the special election. He hoped it would be. Thomas was a good man, and he'd be good for the City of Baltimore.

Thomas put on his hat, and tipped the brim toward them before leaving. After he'd gone, the three of them sat at the table, eating, each lost in his own thoughts. Finally, Tony pushed his plate away. "So, I believe I promised you two a stipend. You performed tremendously well last night, perfect in every detail. You fulfilled your end of the bargain; I'm honor bound to discharge mine." He held his cup up for Mama to refill with piping hot coffee. "I had one thousand dollars each in mind. That should be more than enough to set you up comfortably in whatever city you choose, be it New York, Baltimore, or elsewhere."

Seamus and Daniel's eyes grew large and round. Seamus was the first to recover use of his tongue. "A thousand dollars? *Each?* Sweet Jaysus, I never had that much money in me life, let alone at one time!"

"A thousand dollars...think of it, Seamus! We could do anything, go anywhere!" Daniel grinned, and his eyes sparkled with excitement. "We could go to Ireland, or to France, or...or to Africa!"

Seamus snorted. "Why would we go to Africa? How would

we even get there?"

"On a boat, I suppose, same as anywhere else. Oh, I don't care where we go. We're rich!" Daniel laughed with delight, and bounced in his chair like an excited child.

Tony frowned at them and wagged a finger. "I don't want to lecture you two, but this is your one chance at making decent lives for yourselves. Don't waste it on fancy trips and unnecessary luxuries."

"Aw, we're just funning," Seamus said. "Actually, we was talking, me and Dandy...er, Daniel, about what we wanted to do. See, we think with our powers, we'd make good Pinkerton men."

Tony gaped at them. With all the things he'd thought Seamus and Daniel would do with the money, becoming Pinkerton men didn't even make the list. "You want to be detectives with the Pinkerton Agency?" He looked from one man to the other. "Why?"

"Why not?" Daniel countered. "We was always the bad guys. Thieves and such, I mean. Now we're not. You taught us we can be honest and still get ahead. Besides, after meeting Thomas, we think being detectives would be interesting."

Seamus nodded. "Dandy...er, Daniel—sorry, I keep forgetting—could use his power to help solve the crime, and I could use mine to get back stolen money, or jewelry, or disarm bank robbers. How about it? Will you put in a good word for us, Tony?"

"Well, I don't know anyone at the Pinkerton Agency personally, but I'll be happy to write you both strong letters of recommendation."

Seamus and Dandy beamed, then served themselves up more eggs, sausage, and biscuits. Still talking between themselves about money, cities around the world, and the Pinkerton Agency, they tucked in.

The way they ate, it seemed to Tony they must've never had

more than a passing acquaintance with food before. Mama loved it, though, and refilled the platters as soon as they emptied. She was going to miss those two when they'd moved on.

Tony chuckled to himself and then stood, sticking the newspaper under his arm. "If you need me, I'll be upstairs in my suite. I've some personal business to attend to."

He sat in the overstuffed armchair in his suite, his favorite, the one he kept near the fire but not uncomfortably close to the heat. He was naked, and had one leg draped comfortably over the arm of the chair. He'd poured himself a nice glass of sherry, and was sipping it thoughtfully. It was a mite early in the day to imbibe, perhaps, but he felt he'd more than earned it.

Everything had finally worked out the way he'd planned, and he couldn't be happier. Well, aside from Leopold's untimely death, that is, but they'd avenged him quite efficiently, in Tony's opinion. They'd buried him in Baltimore Cemetery, in a plot paid for by the club. Tony had purchased a small, tastefully carved headstone bearing his birth name—Leopold Hoffman. At the end of the ceremony, just before the diggers began to backfill the grave, Thomas laid a black collar and golden chain on the casket.

Seamus and Daniel had proven themselves dependable, staunch allies in times of crisis, just as he'd hoped when he'd chosen them for his little experiment. Now they would be men of means, perhaps with new jobs as Pinkerton men.

Thomas was now a dear friend, and a trusted member of the club, one whose position in the Baltimore police department— and perhaps, one day, as mayor of the city—would only serve to further protect them all.

Best of all, Tony had proven to himself he was no fluke,

that a man lifted from poverty could make a success of himself given the proper tools and support. It was nurture, not nature, which proved the mettle of a man.

He drained his glass and set it aside, then reached for a small vial of his sandalwood scented oil on the table next to his chair. He uncorked it and poured some into his hand. Putting the bottle back, he slicked his cock, and then settled back in the chair, shifting his weight a bit until he found a more comfortable position. His hand began to work his cock with long, languid strokes.

It felt so good to touch himself, especially without any of the pressures he'd been laboring under lately. No parties to plan, no bodies to bury, just pulling slowly and firmly on his dick. He cupped his balls, gave them a few light tugs, and let out a soft sigh.

When he closed his eyes, a certain young man popped into his head, one with dark hair, swarthy skin, and the brightest blue eyes Tony had yet seen. In his memory, Tony relived the Saturday night before at the party. He saw himself fisting the geycat's ass, and then fucking it. He could practically feel the squeeze of that luscious ass, first around his fingers and then his cock; hear the slap of his hips againstthose plump buttocks, and the wet sounds of his slicked cock fucking a well-prepared hole.

His breathing grew rapid, huffing in and out between his parted lips, keeping time with his rapidly beating heart as his hand worked his cock faster, squeezing it tighter. His balls swelled, full of his need, the first stirrings of his climax beginning to build.

He could almost smell the scent of male seed in the air, and hear the soft moans of the geycat as Tony rode with an almost brutal pace. It had been an exciting encounter, particularly with the audience they'd attracted, far more so than he'd had in quite a while. The excitement of having men watching as he fucked, hearing his noises, smelling his scent, sharpened his desire. Reliving it in his mind was almost as good as doing it in reality, and he came with a series of soft grunts, spilling over his hand.

"Towel, sir?" Walther appeared next to him, proffering a clean square of cotton.

"Thank you, although I've asked you repeatedly not to pop in on me when I'm masturbating. It's off-putting." He took the towel and cleaned himself up, then wiped his hands before handing it back.

Walther took the towel, holding it between the tips of his forefinger and thumb. "Very good, sir. Oh, and his name is Ethan, sir."

"What?"

"Who, not what, sir. Ethan. The young man you, er...used as a human puppet the night of the party." Walther pantomimed shoving his arm up a puppet's rear, then making the puppet talk.

"Why, I never!" Tony sputtered, but soon began to laugh. "A puppet, eh? Good one, Walther."

"Thank you, sir." Walther began to fade away.

"Walther, wait just a moment. The geycat, his name is Ethan, did you say?"

"Yes, sir. He's one of Maude Breem's men. You might find him at the Soiled Dove, I imagine." He winked outas quick as a blink, taking Tony's sticky towel with him.

Tony smiled, and stood up. He walked to the bed where he'd carefully folded his clothes when he'd undressed. He hadn't thought to go outside today, instead wanting to stay in, be lazy, perhaps take a long soak in a hot bath, but now his plans had changed. It seemed he felt the need to pay Maude Breem a visit. It was overdue anyway, he told himself.

Besides, he was curious. How much money, he pondered, would Madam Breem charge to release one of her whores from a contract with her, and would such a young man—say one with dark hair and swarthy skin, and the brightest bluest eyes Tony had ever seen—once freed from his obligations, be amenable to a little experiment? One that might just lift this young man from a life spent earning his living with his mouth and ass into one of respectability, culture, wealth, and refinement?

Tony grinned as he dressed. He slipped into his heavy top-coat, tamped his beaver-felt top hat down on his head, picked up his gold-topped walking stick, and left his suite, all the while whistling a jaunty little tune.

Epilogue

A year had passed since the night of the party at Club Raven.

Seamus and Daniel sat side-by-side on a train headed west. The car was almost empty; there were just two other men and three women, one of which had two rowdy children traveling with her. One the children, a freckle-faced boy, kept turning around and sticking his tongue out at them.

They paid the child little enough mind, preferring to keep their gazes pinned to the scenery rolling by out the smoke-streaked windows.

The first indication that something was wrong came in the form of squealing brakes, and the train shuddering to a sudden stop. The women screamed, and the men harrumphed, and the children cried—well, one did. The other had been sticking his tongue out at them when the train braked and had nearly bitten it off.

Outside the train, men raced by on horseback, kerchiefs pulled up over their mouths and noses. They raced toward the engine, horses kicking up clots of dirt.

"Think it's the Red Eye Gang?" Seamus craned his neck, trying to see past Daniel to the outlaws galloping past.

"Don't know. They're not wearing signs."

"That mouth of yours is going to get you in trouble yet, Dandy."

"It's Daniel, and you didn't find anything wrong with me mouth last night." Daniel smirked, then stuck his head out of the window. "Whoever they are, they've got the engineer out of the cab. We should be movin', boyo."

Seamus nodded. "How many?"

"I counted six men. Two with shotguns, and four with revolvers, two each in hip holsters."

"Good. Let's go."

They ran through the car, slammed open the door and jumped off the train, racing alongside it to where the desperadoes were trying to deal with an engineer and a guard who were reluctant to give up the key to the safe containing a fortune in gold being sent west.

"Boys, best give yourselves up now."

"Who the fuck are you?"

"The name is Seamus O'Brian, and this is me good friend, Daniel Gilroy." He held out a golden badge that glittered in the sunlight, and pointed a revolver at them. "We're Pinkerton men, and you're under arrest, buckos."

The men looked at one another and laughed. "There's six of us, asshole, and only two of you. We've got you outgunned."

"Guns?" Seamus looked confused. "Oh, you mean those over there?" He moved slightly to the left, exposing a pile consisting of two shotguns and eight revolvers. "I believe we're the ones who have *you* outgunned."

The expressions on their faces when they reached for their weapons and found them gone, was priceless. Seamus laughed out loud.

Daniel walked over to the pile of weapons, always careful to keep his gun trained on the men just in case Seamus had missed one, then stooped down and touched the shotgun that lay on the top of the heap. "It's them, Seamus. The Red Eye Gang. They just robbed a bank in Cheyenne just a week ago. Shot three people in cold blood—the bank manager and two tellers."

Seamus clucked his tongue at them. "Tsk, tsk. You're naughty boys, ain't you? Now, move slow, because I sure would hate to have to shoot you. Oh, wait, no, I'm lying. I'd be as happy as a leprechaun who shat gold if I got to shoot you."

"I want to shoot one, too, Seamus. That one, the big one with the scar on his plug ugly face. It's his shotgun I touched. He raped a woman a couple of weeks ago in Independence, then slit her throat."

The man Daniel spoke about twitched his hand, and Daniel's gun went off, bucking slightly in his hand. Acrid smoke tickled their noses, except for the rapist. He was laid out in the dirt, a neat hole in his forehead. "Oops."

"Anybody else want to be stupid?" Seamus motioned with his gun. "Down on the ground, hands behind your backs, boys."

Daniel looked over at Seamus as he finished securing handcuffs on the last of the Red Eye Gang's wrists. "Tony would be proud of us, yeah?"

"I'm sure of it, boyo. We'll have to write him and tell him about this one, though. He'll enjoy hearing it." Seamus stood and hauled the robber to his feet. "See, just a year ago we was in Five Points, just two lowborn pickpockets. Now look at us, Pinkerton men on the right side of the law." He pushed the desperado toward the train where he'd be joining the others of his gang for their ride into nearest city with a circuit court judge. "Ain't you lucky you ran into us now instead of then? Why we might've picked your pockets clean. Right, Dandy?"

"Right you are, Bull."

Thomas Arthur Clare placed his hand on the Bible and swore the oath of office as mayor of the City of Baltimore. He'd won in the special election after Gideon Forge's death, and had again in the regular election.

Contrary to what he'd told Tony soon after that cold night when Leopold had been killed, he was interested in being mayor. He might have to learn as he went, but he certainly couldn't do any worse than his predecessor.

As it turned out, Gideon Forge had been thoroughly corrupt right down to the black, withered heart beating in his chest. He'd been stealing money from the city treasury for years, as well as taking kickbacks, bribes, and exhorting money from city businessmen for protection from, evidently, himself.

It had been a long, hard year, though. Thomas had to weed out crooked cops from the force, firing some and arresting others, putting them in their own jail for offenses ranging from assault and battery to extortion. There were dishonest civilian employees as well, guilty of running crooked dice games in the City Hall basement, illegal lotteries, and taking bets on bare-knuckle fights.

He made it through the year without incurring too many scars due largely in part to Club Raven and to Tony, who'd talked to Maude Breem and found Thomas another Dom. Marcos was different from Leopold—kind, quiet, but with a firm hand, and just as intuitive about Thomas's needs. He'd learned to trust Marcos, although it had taken much longer than it had with Leopold. He'd learned that lesson hard but well.

On a happier note, he'd learned to keep a pillow on his office chair for the days after he visited the club.

Mama slid a plate of veal parmesan in front of Tony. "*Mangia, Antonio. Sei troppo magro.*"

Tony sighed. "I am eating, Mama, and for the last time, I'm not too skinny. You just want to make me fat."

"Fat, fat...meat on the bones is good. No woman wants a skinny man."

Tony arched an eyebrow at her. "YourEnglish is improving, Mama. Walther must be a good teacher." He purposely didn't address the *no woman wants* remark. No sense in fighting that battle unless necessary.

"Bah." She smirked at him and bustled off, already distracted by her responsibilities in feeding the staff at Club Raven.

Tony smiled, and cut off a piece of veal. He chewed, but the meat practically melted in his mouth. He took a sip of Cabernet and sighed. Life was sweet here at Club Raven. He had his mama's cooking, good friends, and the company, however temporary, of a lovely dark-haired, swarthy skinned man with the most brilliantly blue eyes he'd ever seen.

If anyone's life wasbetter than this, he'd surely like to see it.